D1516920

V A N

G O G H ' S

B A D

C A F É

Tintin in the New World

Tallien: A Brief Romance

The Adventures of Mao on the Long March

VAN GOGH'S BAD CAFÉ

a love story

Frederic Tuten

William Morrow and Company, Inc.

New York

It is the policy of William Morrow and Company, Inc., and its
imprints and affiliates, recognizing the importance of preserving
what has been written, to print the books we publish on acid-free
paper, and we exert our best efforts to that end.

Library of Congress Cataloging-in-Publication Data

Tuten, Frederic.
    Van Gogh's bad café : a love story / Frederic Tuten.
        p.   cm.
    ISBN 0-688-15134-5
    1. Gogh, Vincent van, 1853-1890—Fiction.   I. Title.
PS3570.U78V36   1997
813'.54—dc21   96-29649
                                                CIP

Printed in the United States of America

First Edition

1   2   3   4   5   6   7   8   9   10

BOOK DESIGN BY FRITZ METSCH

All the artwork was created expressly
for this novel by Eric Fischl.

I dedicate this novel, with love, to the memory of John Resko (1911–1991). ''The trees were so close I could smell them and the road began singing to me.''

We ought not be awake. It is from this
That a bright red woman will be rising.

WALLACE STEVENS

Half measures availed us nothing. . . .

THE BIG BOOK

VAN

GOGH'S

BAD

CAFÉ

It was different then. You could be standing by a burned-out lot, waiting for no one and nothing, not even for a lonely red bus. You'd be just there, studying the rubble of a building along Avenue C. Charred bricks and shrieking plasterboard, a bathtub naked on its side, and through its drain, a lone sunflower, sulfuric yellow and furred like a honeybee screwing upward toward a whirling yellow sun.

Standing there at that corner, you could say hello to the wildest strangers as they passed you by, because down there, we were all loose change tripping the streets, the coins falling where they may, liberty dimes and buffalo nickels mixing promiscuously, without a thought, on some blue curb below Tenth Street.

"Hi, Jack. Hi, Jill." You'd give a little salute, and most times, they'd wave back or smile or come over and ask about where to crash, about where to score, sometimes just to have a chat with a stranger. We recognized who we were at a glance—all irregulars from the drifting nation of dreamy youth. We're ghosts of those times now, just nicked, straight-edged razors heaped in pawnshop drawers. Don't get old. Don't die. Kill despair. Keep hope.

How easily flowed the day in those old times, when I was most alive, my blood running casually and forever. I'd be letting the hours pass in a drowse, drinking, sleeping, now and then shooting pictures for love and for the truth in them, every frame a hedge against oblivion, the never having lived—I believed things like that in those days.

I used to sit away an afternoon in Mousey's Bar—vanished now—on Avenue C and drink slowly through the day until evening hit the pavement. In those days, I'd bring Mousey my check and take a few dollars in cash for walking money and film stock, and leave him the rest for me to draw against the bar. The bar being my endless draw, calling me to my little round table by the window where I could read and look out on the street and go off and take a walk—and maybe shoot a roll of river and clouds—and return to find my cozy drink still waiting.

One killing, late July day, too hot to stay in Mousey's, I headed down to the East River to cool off and sit some while on my slatted green bench, facing the traffic of tugs and barges and all the giant freighters and the smaller floating life easing to and fro in the river's breeze. I'd go sit there under a sickly elm tree and imagine other rivers and their cities that I'd one day photograph. On that bench I would dream many things.

But I started dreaming even before I got to my bench, my head woozy and hot. The blaze of sun bakes your brains, unless you're wearing a straw hat with a high crown, one reaching to grate the belly of a sluggish cloud, say. I was hatless and on my way to my river bench, taking a shortcut across a rubble-filled lot of a burned-out building on Avenue C, when I saw before me a clean, free-standing brick wall in the middle of the debris.

I had my camera out now, but not to shoot just another photo of a wall standing high in the rubble of an empty lot—plasterboard jutting like jagged ice floes among the splintered beams of a four-master smashed in the glistening sun of an arctic crush, a bathtub, beached among the flotsam, naked on its side, with an infant cypress tree spearing through its drain hole. Not the wall, but a movement within it captured me, the midday sun overhead blanching my vision so that all I saw was the center of the wall cleaving, slowly forming a pout of lips.

Something was parting through the lips and stepping its way out of the wall, a she. I thought it was the sun piercing through the crown of my head again, its spiking rays ready to fix me to the heavy ties of the earth while its white light blinded my eyes and heart. I'd just be lying there convulsing, waiting for the thieves to come and lift the change from my pockets and the camera from my belly. "Dig this fucker. What's that shit in his mouth, come?"

Me writhing there, humiliated, getting robbed, sightless among the pavement's sparkles, with that little fit inspired by the sun. But that fit didn't come over me. She did, out from the parting slit in the wall.

She walked toward me smiling, at ease among shards and rubble, as if treading the sweet moss of her private green pasture, ruling the turf and all life below its sky, her narrow shoulders pulled square and high, her hair a tangled cinnamon-red bush, a fiery red thicket. She throws back her head, pausing to address her shepherd. *"Où est Louis? Où est-ce que c'est toi qui l'as?"*

Another French kid, I thought. The kind who likes it down here in the alphabet avenues where the snow lasts all through winter and summer, hills of snow covering the grass in Tompkins Square Park and spilling over into the gutters. Even at the most raw locations they step politely, these folk, having been taught from birth to wipe their shoes on the doormat before touring the madhouse.

I did not know where Louis was. I did not know any Louis she might know.

"And you, is it that you have of it, perhaps?" she asks, still smiling and now in English.

The dodo! For her, I could have of it the anything she desired, perhaps. But she desired, as she quickly let me know, the morphine. Not my genre of dreams, the morphine. Me always trying to keep sober, but mostly slipping, fearing, and wanting to fall. No matter how I tried, I was still nursing my bottle at Mousey's, and sipping tequila alone at my apartment late at night when the lonely walls needed speaking to.

"And what of cocaine?" she inquires.

"Non plus," I answer, testing the range of my French.

Quel disappointment on her face. More beautiful, more blue-eyed, more the adolescent than when she stepped through the wall just moments before. I went up and down a little list, curious to test whether she cared for other druggy possibilities. Of speed, speedballs, V's, Quaaludes, your general stock of uppers and downers, angel dust, meth, dollies, heroin, crack, she did not sing. Glue, paint thinner, marinated old socks, not a warble. Not very à la mode, she. Didn't even know what I was talking about, though I could see I was amusing her with my jargon, the lingo I had picked up in the street of dated novels.

No, morphine. That was her simple dope. The drug of yesteryear, where she seemed just to have stepped out from: heavy green divans, palm plants in blue porcelain pots, thick purple brocade curtains snuffing out the light and air from the street, the city, the world; candles flickering wearily their anemic *fin de siècle* flames; she's splayed on the bed, pillows puffed about her, on the night table a crystal of water laced with laudanum—for the nerves; on a silver tray, a single lily in a lilac vase, a syringe, its blood-flecked needle still moist, warm. She's drowsy, half asleep, smiling, dreamy. She's dreaming in a century poised for its end, and she floats in its embrace as it carries her over the bridge of human time to the brink of another century's death.

We walk. Her dress, long, white, and cinched at the narrow waist, a late-nineteenth-century costume from an antique store (gone now) on Avenue B and Tenth Street, maybe. I'm dressed in the common rags of the day, heavy-soled boots made to last, khaki trousers baggy and thick—as I wear them in all seasons—a blue cotton shirt with pockets wide enough to harbor a small trunk, a carpenter's shirt I'd bought from the Salvation Army store.

No morphine. And thus, no transactions or conversation between us of the druggy or of any sort. Leaving, for the moment, the grounds of our discourse to retreat out there where parallel lines marry, leaving us to walk side by side, already an old, affectionate couple, with the open day spread before us to fill as we liked.

I was ready to walk all the compass points, each direction another hope-filled prospect stretching to the end of our lives. I was ready, already, to live with her and share the common dish, to make children—should she want—and bring home the bacon, if need be, and share the daily fate, even boredom, and to keep with her to death and in the reaches beyond, twin spirits holding hands up there in a sky of stars and planets, or to become a pair of companionate hawks in our iron love nest atop the Brooklyn Bridge.

Or for love's mad sake, I'd drink with her at Mousey's or even at home. Matching shot for shot. Day and night drinking, and early dawn drinking, and watch her shoot morphine 'til room and bed and street and the tip of Manhattan spun off into the Atlantic and floated away to deposit us in France, or from whatever fairyland she had come.

"Where we going?" I ask, noticing she has my hand and that we are walking in circles.

She shrugs. *"Sais pas."*

"Come with me, then," I say.

"Why not." Her English was improving with each step. "You are a gentleman, I conceive."

"Perhaps," I say. "And you, if you're a crazy woman, tell me now, because I'm ill from crazy persons."

When she speaks, she doesn't look into my face or eyes, she's already won them. It's my little Minolta that's fascinated her. Does she want it, and my dollars, too, I wonder? But her regard does not last very long, she's soon marveling at the street and the buildings and at the river beyond us.

Without my realizing it, we're standing in front of Mousey's, where, I suggest, we step in for a drink. She makes a clicking sound and shakes her head.

"Let us go *chez toi.*"

Ah! now I get the drift. She wants to hook me,

this loony angel. So what, I think. I'd rather drown swimming in her than flap around free, my gills burning in the solitary air. So now we swim the blocks, she a graceful sidestroke, dress streaming in the airy flow, me doing the dog paddle, house keys between my teeth.

We're *chez moi, tout de suite,* top floor, under the hot tar roof, and into my broiling crèche, furnished with miraculous simplicity, a chair for myself and another for company, and ample enough to accommodate a sluggish cat and his companion mouse.

Her smile's gone. The shoulders cave in slightly. A morsel of disappointment crosses her lips.

Is it that she does not like my flat?

"Pas du tout. It has its negligent charm. A little like Vincent's," she says sleepily.

Her face collapses as she says that. I show concern. But nothing is wrong, she adds reassuringly. I should not derange myself for her. Only, she's *un peu fatiguée.* She's grown tired. From our little stroll under the hammering sun, perhaps? Or from climbing the six-flight walk-up?—each landing a plateau of checkered linoleum clouds. Or is she spent from her trip through the wall or from wherever else her journey had begun?

Oh, *oui, bien sûr,* she's *vraiment fatiguée* and desiring a bath. (Which she'd postpone, of course, and take sometime later, if I would only conduct her to certain desirable stuff.)

The architects of the tenements down here had

planned it so that the poor may dine and bathe at the same time; the bathtub's planted in the kitchen, for convenience's sake. I quarter fill it, too nervous to wait for the drowsy water to climb higher on its porcelain wall, and fearful she might suddenly freshen up and, with the same whim that had decided her to visit me, now wish to vanish from me. But there's no need to fear. In a zip, she undresses before my eyes. She's a mass of underclothes—no wonder she's tired. Who wouldn't suffer heat exhaustion from all those petticoats and shifts, camisoles and clothy things? Eventually, she strips down to her true size. Skinny size. Long-limbed and smooth—youth-sized and immortal.

I take her with my eyes, then step toward her with my arms stiffly extended. But she shrugs her squared shoulders, as if to say, "Friend, be calm, go easy, I'm not here for you." And I back off, thinking, Yes, of course, now that she's here, we have all the world's time, a slow decade or two before us.

She slips into the tub and motions for me to wash her. I soap and sponge her down, the milky water flowing down her creamy neck and shoulders, trickling over her needle-tracked thin flanks. It's clear to me now that I was washing away the film of her past, the apricot patina of the nineteenth century.

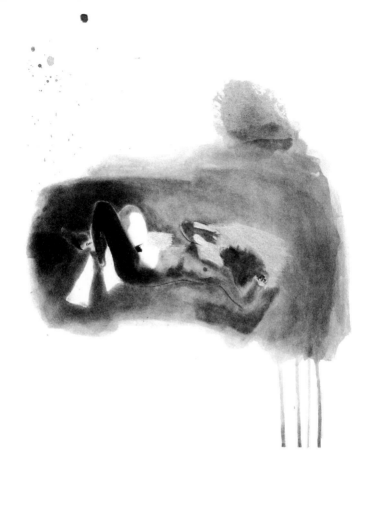

Chapter 2

We sleep and nap and laze in bed—my two piled-up mattresses on the bare wooden floor. We are silent, dreamy. She surveys my photographs crowded on the wall. I have no particular subject, no special theme. The Brooklyn Bridge at dawn will do, tugs and their milky wake, elms fading in the fading light, my postman and his green mailbag. It's the shooting that excites me. Printing is the fatiguing task after action, the dressing of the game after the hunt. (Not that I've done either.) I have no patience for the care it takes. So indifferent am I that I leave rolls of undeveloped film scattered on the floor, in the sleeves of pillows, under and on the bed— lumps of shot film prodding me in the silence of dawn.

"They are not seasoned," she says, nodding to the photos. The postman, the elms, the bridges, the self-portraits in the bureau mirror, all so many unripe fruits cut prematurely from the vine. The work was unseasoned, not yet complete.

It was a brief trial and her verdict was in. I knew she was right, but still it hurt, as when you're caught in a lie you did not wish to tell. Could I tell her, so soon, that I was lost to myself, negligent of the concentration I needed to ripen my work and to bring my blurry self into focus? I was still in my thirties, burning to live but fearful of fire, fearfilled and living by halves, while life requests full measure.

Having passed judgment, she continues looking about the room, stopping at a van Gogh print that I had taped to the wall above my bed. She springs up to it, her fingers caressing the surface. She cries out, alarmed by who knows what.

"It's Marguerite," she says catching her breath, "but it's not a painting."

"I store the original in a Swiss vault," I said.

"And how did you obtain a copy of Vincent's painting?"

"From a shop, where everyone gets them," I answer with a deliberate sigh of exasperation at her make-believe antics.

Impossible. She had seen it just the other day. It was drying in Vincent's room. No. She corrected herself. The canvas was in Dr. Gachet's house. The doctor so loved his daughter's portrait that he took it from Vincent and hung it unframed and still wet.

She's dwelling on the puzzle of this picture calmly. She would have to clear up this affair when she saw Vincent again—very soon, as he was probably, in fact, most assuredly, anxiously waiting—to understate his condition—for her this very moment.

"Waiting for you, where?" I ask.

She smiles. My interest excites her power. She has a little hook into my nether lip and is testing how far to let the line run free before making the strike.

Vincent was, should I wish to know, at this very moment, searching for her at the Bad Café, or perhaps he was in one or another corner of his fields—probably the one near the church he liked to paint—pretending to work while worrying himself to distraction over her.

"You must be very special for Vincent to worry so much about you," I say.

"I am the thing he likes most best," she answers matter-of-factly. Vincent, her pup, her kitten, her drunken red goose.

She's yawning now and getting cranky. Soon she'll be sick. What have I got stored at home— no more jokes, she says—some cocaine, perhaps? She'd even accept some hashish, though she didn't like it very much. A veteran of the French campaigns in Algeria was a hashish man and smoked it all day long; they had smoked together in her garden, but she did it more to keep him company than for the pleasure of the thing itself.

No more jokes, I say. I had nothing home for her except myself, who desired that she stay or at least spend the night, in whatever manner or terms she wished.

She gives me a friendly smile. Yes, as she had

supposed, I was a gentleman. Indeed, so. And she liked me, too. Another defective, she could tell. The soul in damage, like a glove with the fingertips cut off, and the palms, too. But, even with all of that, she must be leaving. She is collecting herself, dressing lazily, her brief house visit (and bath) was reaching its formal conclusion.

Yes, she'd have to leave and go home soon.

And where is that?

To Auvers, naturally—as if I should know— the town where she and Vincent live. In their sweet little Auvers-sur-Oise, she adds wistfully, just some kilometers' distance, but, oh!, so far away from Paris. The calm of trees and fields and river, her garden. Vincent, he'd be there waiting for her, missing her profoundly, she says, her voice deepening very far, deep into the pit of her and traveling miles away from us both. Vincent. Yes, she missed him, too—"that strange tremble of a man."

"Ah, Louis," she exclaims, stung by some image I vaguely see filmed in her eyes, "you should only know of what strong iron he is made. He is not of the stuff of whoever you and I are. When he comes to my gate, I do not need ask, 'What have you brought me?'—when he makes me, without his knowing it—and that is his powerful charm—the present of himself."

She is far away again, where slow mirrors fracture time and send up little puffs of drowsy smoke. Vincent and she, already like an old couple, although they had known each other only some few weeks, sixty-three days, not counting when she first set eyes on him that time in the hospital in Saint-Rémy, and not counting when she followed him after he arrived at Auvers-sur-Oise, she hiding behind a tree while he was painting in a field, such a freckled white man, with hair so red—though not as thick as hers—alone in that field, his white shirt open at the throat, painting. Even when he was in that hospital he was painting—and brooding, and trying to smile, but it was only the smile of a lonely man forcing himself to be brave while his heart sank down in his chest. She herself was acquainted with that smile, having smiled it herself, everywhere, exactly where loneliness lived.

It was that smile and his painting and his clothes that spoke to her before she knew who he was or ever thought she would see him again after she left the hospital. Workingman's clothes, rough and made of spun iron, and his worker's boots, cleanly oiled and old and tired of life, having walked up and down the stony, broken paths by smooth roads where the poor and other outcasts were not invited to walk and where he had chosen to walk among them.

She had gone home to her subject now, was dwelling beside it: her Vincent. My Scheherazade of the needle is weaving her yarn with her eyes half-closed, her voice a long line spinning about my heart, binding me to her.

She yawns. Revives, drowsily. Then recommences. Vincent is her *homme raté,* her failure of a man. He failed at everything, even at being a preacher, and who can fail at that?—excepting mutes. She looks in my eyes. Then down along the tracks on the inner cream of her thighs, her fingers patting the needle trail.

"Don't worry, later," I say, lying. Later we'll go out and she can buy all she wants, anything she would like out there where the streets branch into tin and cardboard coves, dens with splintery orange crates for chairs, barbed wire laid out for carpets, whirling arc lamps burning in the charcoal night.

In time we'd go out, I promised, and out there in the night we'd find her the sleeping juice she wants or maybe we'd even sail down to Mousey's and drink behind closed after-hours doors until dawn draws us out to bake us in the morning sun. She weighs my promises against her wish to sleep or leave and search for herself in the unknown streets the stuff she wanted or to return to where she had started, somewhere in that country place with her Vincent. The scale finally favors her stay with me. And she returns to her tale, her telling it a reassuring anchor to her faraway home.

I'm again in her weave, but I now keep watch to straighten the thread of her lines, helping sometimes even to shape her wayward design. And soon I'm far in it, inseparable from it, taking her story for my own, leaving behind the menaces of the day, leaving Mousey's and the river bench and the burning streets streaming to it. Leaving my old life behind, burning in the walls and flaming on the tar roof above my head.

I'm at the iron gate of Ursula's cottage in Auvers-sur-Oise, heart pounding, waiting beside Vincent to enter. And now I'm with that man at her door, his hand a bit shaky, his red hair patted down and wet, his face burnished and expectant.

Chapter 3

Her pathway, twisting and red. It staggered through a green garden and halted at an iron gate topped by wavy spearheads—tips of cypress trees in an iron breeze. Vincent stood at her gate, his hand on the latch.

Ursula was inside the cottage just beyond the gate, but she herself was always outside the pale, beyond the safe perimeter, dozing someplace in wild territory where Vincent could not protect her, could not keep her from the outlaw self who called her to forests whose roots lead to the grave.

The cottage door was left open, a good sign that she was awake and—as she had said in her note that she would be—waiting for him.

She rose gravely from the green sofa to meet him as he half stumbled into the white room. In one sweep she pressed against him, putting her hand about the nape of his neck, her head on his chest. He kissed the tangle of her red hair, her cheek, holding her tightly. She pressed herself to him as if to enter some waiting cove of his person.

They did not speak but went directly to her bed. She called out his name, her voice, the wolf's low, white murmur, taking them to dens where once they had nested after the hunt, her coat flecked with dry snow and blood and strips of fern. Vincent let out a sigh, Ursula a long sniffle.

Some moments later, they spoke about a blue Chinese cup they had seen in a Paris shop window, Vincent admiring the bridge floating over a misty chasm and the mountains in a soft distance. The artist who had designed that image had no name; Vincent's name boldly decorated his paintings, the signature his only vanity, Ursula said, tenderly taking his hand. And hand in hand they slept through the afternoon heat, Vincent waking first in the minty shade of evening.

Later, in the garden, Ursula read to him in a clearing spread with blankets. Straw sombrero sloped over his face, his arms hoisted above his head, his legs spread apart, Vincent, half dreaming yet alert to her, visualized her with book in hand, her hair playing over the pages.

What was she reciting? Was she really reading or was she speaking to her garden plants and herbs, her rooted children as she had called them? To speak to plants had its charms—because all is forgiven the young, even their raptures and posturing. But now Vincent imagined Ursula poor and old, the town's old loon with weeds and straws in her brittle red hair, her youth and beauty no longer shields against the contempt shown the aged and powerless. Who would take care of her when he was under the earth?

Ursula was reading to him in English now, the language of her other self—Jack's tongue.

" 'You are very beautiful to me, you faintly tinged roots—you make me think of death, Death is beautiful from you (What indeed is beautiful, except Death and Love?), O I think it is not for life I am chanting here my chant of lovers—I think it must be for death. . . .' "

"It must not be for death, no," Vincent said, raising himself on his elbows. "Sing for the living and for life, sing for the joy of our time here in your garden."

She put her book in her lap and squinted at him as if he were a marmalade cat she happened upon in a cemetery on the moon.

"When you go to buy it in Paris," she said, finally, "where you think they would not have time for such sport—they make you wait and wait to humiliate you, to make you feel low, so that you want even more to rid yourself of yourself and the bad things you feel."

The old song again. She was rehearsing it. Unless he could stop her, she would mount into a full dirge, the furious mourning song of her desire.

"Stop now," Vincent said almost harshly. "Stop before you drown in your own poison."

That would be good. To drown in it. Sink down into the River Lethe and sleep forever in its timeless flow. But he had misunderstood her, as usual, had impoverished her meaning—and had, in fact, spoken, much unlike him, vulgarly. Not death she craved, but sweet completion.

"What you call addiction, Vincent, I call desire. The plant desires the sun; roots, water. My nerves desire certain stuff to bring them to quietude."

"As when you lie there on your pillow, stiff and dead?"

"I like being that way," she said. "I even like getting sick from time to time and throwing up. Maybe God loves my vomit, Vincent."

She invited a response. Waited for Vincent to say his lines. He held back for fear of bringing the matter to where she could—and would—find in his words reason to flare into a tantrum of self-justification. He knew that the longer he paused, the stronger her fury when finally he spoke, but Vincent was caught dumb.

"At least have the courtesy of recognizing me, allow me that little dignity, Monsieur."

Ah! It was *Monsieur,* again, the word that signaled her further cries of war.

"There is no need to quarrel," he answered finally. "Sit beside me and let me hold you."

She would allow, reluctantly, however, being held, as long as Vincent understood that she was not surrendering to him—to do so would be false of her since she was still—and for however long she did not know—angry with him. So Vincent held her, his free hand gently masking her eyes from the world.

She was calming again now, but ever so slowly, so would he please not speak or breathe too apparently, for she was on the way to composing her thoughts and to seeing them with clarity. And with the aid of this clarity a plan was forming, an old one, a plan whose direction was the West. She would go away, as she always had said she would, to the West, where, if he remembered, she would join Geronimo, Sitting Bull, Crazy Horse, Buffalo Bill, Calamity Jane, and Billy the Kid. She would ride with them and gallop far away to the plains and the prairies and the pistols.

There she would shoot and shoot. And one day, when she had her own ranch and her loyal band of cowboys and cowgirls, that one day she'd send for him. Vincent would then be free to paint the western skies and the cottonwoods and the hills dotted with wild cactus—and their sprouting spiked pink roses—as beautiful as any field of hay or stand of cypresses he was so fond of. Wait! A new and better plan was rising from the dreamy fumes of a moment ago.

Still the West, but she'd get rid of the ranch and its attendant burdens—the mending of broken fences and frayed lariats, the breaking of the willful and stubborn cowboys always ready to challenge her authority and to show her up as an ignorant city girl, a Frenchie, to boot—and she'd take the errand of protecting creatures hunted to extinction. She'd be their Diana, hunting those who hunted them, hunting men, running them down, shooting them, their eyes slipping from their sockets with fear, and she'd catch them and gut them still alive and string them up on cottonwood branches as warning to others who would murder bears and buffalo and deer, who would slaughter wolves crooning on hills and sparrows nesting on purple clouds.

Slaughter her enemies, nature's foes. That was her way: to find in the cover of love an excuse for blood. Now she was coming close to drawing his blood; Vincent could feel it coming, the little savage stabs aimed nowhere but at him and the world or at the world through him.

"You see, Vincent, in the West, you'll learn to ride and rope things. You will toughen up, and maybe your paintings will profit from it."

She was out of her dream and had returned to her life.

"Yes," she added, "and perhaps you'll purge your paintings of sentimentality—your greatest flaw, if you forgive my saying."

What had he not forgiven her? he wanted to ask. But what she said had stung him—his flowers twisting to the sun, his wheat fields bent in a driving icy rain, his night skies simmering with stars above black cypresses swaying down to their roots—sentimental, all. Which meant his feelings, too, were sentimental, unexamined and clichéd, his art nothing but postcards crowded with exclamations on wonders natural and touristical. Look at life! Look at life!

"I say this, Vincent, with all regard for what is noble about your work, and with all regard for you."

He needed a respite from such regard, himself so tired from its struggles that he wanted at times to lie in the bushes at the road's edge and sleep 'til time finally burst its rivets and eternity poured through the open seams.

"Monsieur Vincent, drunk again!" a passerby might say, seeing him stretched out at the road's edge. But he would not be drunk. He'd be sleeping until God woke him and announced a fresh day, the rising of a new world from which pain had fled and suffering along with it, too, leaving beauty and love alone to range over the earth.

The sun was leaving the day, its last light arching through the crack between earth and sky. *Entre chien et loup,* as the French call that indistinguishable moment of dusk. That was the light she wished most to photograph—her light of indeterminacy. The light impossible to capture, no matter how wide she opened her camera's lens, no matter how long she waited to shoot it at the last fraction of its life. She could not capture it, that indeterminate light. Darkness she got, instead, a plateful of it, or, at best, some streaks and wisps of white on a smoky glass sheet.

Failures, these plates, and somewhat narrow in intent, Vincent had thought. To winnow the world down to a branch of light, as if that branch spoke for the whole living tree stretching every way to air and sun and marrying the thick sea of earth below. But she had to find her own way, because all else was received, and not born from her.

And there was a longing in her that Vincent revered, as he had said many times to his drink, to the moon, to his boots as he laced them in the dawn. She was often lazy, willful, and spoiled, though she had never been pampered like other beautiful daughters of the rich, but in her art she reached beyond herself and beyond the means of her craft.

"The body and the camera, Vincent, so cumbersome and so limited in what they see, just shells—only the grossest stuff."

"You might as well try to trap moonlight in a cardboard box," Vincent answered, on first seeing her new photographs. To capture an image for the inexpressible, how well he knew that ambition and the strange shivers it gave. Yet Ursula also reached beyond the means of equipment—perhaps even, though time would tell that or not, even her medium.

He had never imagined that one day Ursula would turn to him, photographic plate in hand (in both hands, actually, for that is how large the plates were) and announce that she was finished with photographing the herbs and plants in her garden, done forever with such banal subject matter. For even when she had worked hard to remove the familiar from her picture, familiar it remained—a cloying anecdote.

Vincent was now to understand—and to appreciate—that these passages of light on her glass plates, these fragile marks that translated themselves on printing paper as ribbons and shreds of blankness wedged between blocks of blackness, these were her art. Art finally undecorated by sentiment, free from human rhetoric—art pure.

And now, in her garden, she turned to him. Vanished was the West and the manhunts of hunters; gone, too, her criticism of his paintings, because, look! at this moment, her exact light was forming for her to photograph, and Vincent must rush and get her camera and accompany her to the hill behind the church where she could shoot the expanse of the field right down to the horizon and catch the light as the darkness clamped down on it.

Vincent had to hurry and march with her to her station on the hill—and he had to carry her huge camera for her and the large plates, too, immediately, before the world changed over to night. And so he ran to the shed where she kept her equipment and where she made, through those magic chemical baths, the transformations from the invisible to the manifest world. Her alchemy: the same that had transformed him from Dutch clay to an animal in love.

Returning with her huge camera on his back and the photographic plates in his arms, he followed her as quickly as he could as she raced up the road to the squat Romanesque church and to the field behind it, the very field where he had painted a day earlier, and there, following her instructions, he placed the camera on its three long wooden legs and watched her disappear under the camera's black mantel while the light was crumbling to particles, taking away the trees and the field and the very hill on which they stood, taking away even himself and the shrouded, five-legged creature which had been standing before him only seconds ago.

"It's going," Ursula shouted, her cry muffled by the heavy hump of cloth. "Help me, Vincent."

Help her, to do what? To hold her about the legs, anchor her to the whirling earth, so that she and camera remain fixed to do their difficult work. On his knees he fell, clutching her about her long skirt, holding her and holding his breath, the light turning to motes in the sky. Like a sailor in a gale, Ursula tilted earthward, trying to meet the last light melting behind the horizon. Downward she went, she and camera arching to the earth, until Vincent could no longer keep his hold, Ursula's long skirt slipping under his grasp. With a cry of triumph or of despair—Vincent could not tell which—the hooded creature crashed to the ground in an explosion of metal and glass.

Chapter 4

Vincent walked with Ursula. He, Frankenstein's red-haired creature, with the sweet
child's hand in his mitt, the field of wild flowers
parting before them as they stepped down the
dark glistening glade and into a cove of red pop-
pies and poplars beyond. The creature's in love.
Flower, good. Sky, good. Little Ursula, good. Lift
little Ursula high. Lift to the sky. Oh! Little Ursula cries, and monster tries to kiss her to make
happy again. But this only scares her more and
she begins to howl and let gush the waterworks.
Vincent puts his hand to her wet cheek to comfort her, but she howls the louder and Vincent
doesn't know what to do. Soon he's speaking to
her in Dutch, his own language, his language of
recourse—and he's blabbering the kind of gib-
berish jack-o'-lanterns' palaver on Halloween,
calling to one another across the dark, mown
fields under a frosty pumpkin moon.

Ursula screams loudly enough to wake a grave-
yard of dead drunks. Villagers come running. The

creature does not mistake their waving scythes and flails for peace palms and he lumbers off in a panic of fear and sadness.

All the creature wants is to walk his lady in field and pasture in glen and dale, in the little green byways where thoughts of amour and their attendant sighs and flutterings flourish. No such happiness for Vincent. Ursula was having a fit of nerves, hysteria leaking from the pores, draining the life from her in dark tides.

She had only bruised herself in the fall. But something in her had cracked, along with the smashed plates and the shrouded camera, and had let into the opening a familiar sorrow born before childhood, when the living seeds of what was to be her had taken from the world its dominant themes, catching them as if invisible black rays from the earth and encoding them in her person.

What could he do to calm her?—this Vincent, who had tended the burned bodies of miners brought up from the anthracitic veins of the earth, their picks still frozen in hand, lumps of hot coal glistening in their terrified hair, men screaming and begging for death, eyes and faces scorched in the subterranean explosion, men screaming and begging mother, Christ, and the devil for death.

Vincent had nursed these men, sponging water down their throats, drop by drop. He would have embraced them as they trundled off to eternity would it have helped, would not his hold have parted the steaming flesh from their bones. He survived all of that, taking the pain into himself, swallowing up the screams and flinty burials and the grief of wives and children, until all the backed-up sadness welled up in him and he went berserk in Arles.

But Ursula's plaint, her wail, struck him even deeper than did the screams from the Borinage mines. She was still alive, had not seared nor charred from her grief, but lived, suffering in the unconsuming flames as if indeed on fire, burning. Where did it stem from, her misery? Vincent had no clue. Only its evidence, herself the witness, defendant, and the furious prosecutor in her nervous trial of fire.

They walked home slowly. Vincent with Ursula's camera on his back, the machine's broken legs spiking from his spine. She blubbering, her thin arms hanging by her sides, like a child who thoughtlessly had left behind her favorite dolly on a train speeding to the last stations of the world.

Down the red path, beyond the gate and into the cottage they go; she slides under the thick quilt of the heavy, posted bed and her face is sweet again, her lips in sweet smile. She's safe, in her safe house.

"Vincent, cover me and watch over me all night. Be my night watchman."

Cover her, and at the sign of her crossing over the ledge of sleep, he'd disappear, steal out and return to the Bad Café to down beers and marc in white cups. Her loony fits and loony changes of mood were corroding his happiness with her, driving him back to his old loneliness. He'd escape her for a while and wake in his own hard bed and sip a big bowl of milk-coffee for breakfast and camp in a field with his easel and paint all day. When night fell, he'd stick a candle on the brim of his hat and paint until the wax melted down to flickering stubs and the straw went up in flames, his hair and head along with it—a red-headed man on fire, lighting his palette with his fiery crown.

"Sit in the chair here beside me and fold your hands and watch over me until I wake." Her voice the child's sweet voice, the one going to sleepland far away, where sleepmist sifts through children's bones and makes them forget home.

Vincent positioned himself just as she had wished. She smiled again and shut her eyes, but only for a few moments.

"Are you still here?"

"Forever here."

"Just so, then, Vincent, my knight. For always, two hundred years. 'U' and 'V' side by side, for as long as there's an alphabet."

She turned into the world of her sleep, easing through its soft gates, knowing that Vincent would stand guard to welcome her on her return. So, she slept.

And so, assured she was deep into the realm where Morpheus drowsily presides, Vincent took his deserter's leave and made his way down the hill, seeing through the closed shutters of the Bad

Café rays of greenish red and golden light. He considered pretending to himself that the café was closed for the night—as indeed it was to the ordinary public—and pass it by without looking at the shut door and the golden light that was now flowing under the sill.

He actually passed and went beyond by several feet the door whose golden light was shining in his mind, that light pulling him, conducting him backward to its source. It was a compelling pull, and Vincent finally turned about and marched to the café door. What disappointment in store for him now, should the café indeed be truly closed!

"Fermé, Monsieur." It would be as impersonal as that. As if André, the *patron,* did not know him, had never seen him, never actually had said twenty-two hundred times in the freak hours of the morning, when Vincent was veering to the door, at the edge of his departure, "Ah! Monsieur Vincent, a last and definitive one and then you must let the stars lead you home."

A joke. A jibe. Half the café grinning at the memory of Vincent standing just outside the café door in the middle of the dark morning road, his prick out and leaking piss, his drunken head heavenward—"Little stars lead me home, little lights of God take me there." Vincent's drunken supplication had henceforth found itself mimicked at all hours by the café regulars, their voices pitched to a nasal whine, "Little stars, oh! little stars."

But he need not have feared; the café was not

shut to him. He knocked, and after some still moments, André admitted him. So slowly, however, as to seem an insult. Let in like an extra dog of the night. A smelly wet cur, his paws tracking weeds and sand in the parson's immaculate house.

They were all there, X, Y, and Z, Pissy Marie, her cheeks dripping scarlet rouge, and her man Salvatore, the former convict from Nice, his hands like roast peppers from working in the lye factory, Edouard and Jean and Mathieu, nervous burglars in their cups, others, mere smudges who slumped on their tables, and Louis, trafficker in morphine for those who could not wait out the night for the dispensaries to open their legal trade. Sweet Louis, himself the slave of absinthe, his nose a baby tomato worming with broken veins, his heart gone ashen from want of sunlight and affection. Vincent could not even bring himself to despise this Louis, who, after all, fed Ursula the sleepy poison she craved.

Vincent drank absinthe. Slowly, slowly, slowly, little sips, a laconic baby at the milk breast. Mama's milky green milk, the laced milk of dreaming.

And now he was dreaming: One day, when he was dead, she would be walking in some wonderful land, lanes shouldering through lush lemony fields, she alone, stout, red umbrella under arm, her walk erect—as ever. She would be regarding the field and its crop of yellow boulders with her distracted stare, the stare of the artist asleep to the surface world but awake to the soul of light and all the things that it shapes and shadows. Suddenly, she no longer saw the field or the geometry of its soul; no, it was not anything she had seen in the field that halted her there, alone, her hands a bit thick, in the middle of her tired life.

It was Vincent she saw. His memory returning as a living presence through her. She always had steeled herself against the love of others, until this moment. What had transformed her at exactly this time, so many years after Vincent had gone from her life, himself gone from himself in that tight grave by the living wheat fields?

A man had loved her. A Vincent had loved her. And he was, finally, different from the undifferentiated men and women who had professed their love for her, who had gone, even, to exceptional lengths to demonstrate—by distinguishing acts and passionate strategies—their claims of love. Those lovers and their love, true or not, had rung false to her, their effusions mere steam and burning straw. But Vincent had loved her, was loving her still in the sad ocean of his soul, itself a quick particle in the great soul of the drifting world.

There, in the field, she realized that she had loved him, too, then, so long ago, was loving him still, and that she and Vincent were now joined in their moment, that they were linking, the living and the dead one, forever.

Chapter 5

A boy was watching him. Vincent glimpsed him standing behind a tree or crouched by a boulder, a well-dressed English-looking lad with peaked cap and gray jacket to match his trousers. He was watching Vincent paint. Once, when Vincent paused to light his pipe, their eyes met for an instant, and in that interval the boy fled away in a smooth run. It was the boy who had been staring at him in the Bad Café, the one whom André had made clear, through gesture and grimace, was an odd one—a loon.

The boy resembled another he had seen not too long ago, weeks earlier, in an unhappy world. The asylum in Saint-Rémy, where Vincent was sent after he dug his razor into his head, lopping off a piece of his ear as a souvenir of the attempt. The asylum, with all the other loons and injured, and the boy, too, though Vincent had no idea to which category the youth belonged. And the boy was here now, a reminder of what Vincent had waiting for him should he relapse into despair:

Saint-Rémy or, depending on his finances, a worse place for life, as the doctors at the asylum had threatened should he not stay calm, in control of himself. He'd return to the screams at night and the lime walls with their slits opening to suck him into the other side of the world, a floor of eels waiting to greet him in the foyer.

A beautiful boy had been watching him, and now the boy was gone, and as much as Vincent tried to concentrate on his canvas, he could not. He was not made for boys or their loves; it was not that which had distracted him. The force of youth, the beauty bound in that force, life always fresh, always at dawn, that was what had taken him from his work, from his dream. He, himself, so exhausted from the memories of all that which had drained him. The self remembers everything, Dr. Gachet had told him once, everything you have lived flows in your tissue, living there deeper than the plumb line of your memory.

There was little whose memory did not tire him, drain his hopes, remind him of his failure to share his life with any living thing, though he had once come close to an exchange with God. To have God inside him, as he once had felt when a lay preacher at the Borinage coal mines, to have God waiting to flow through the bridge of his words, but only to find instead God locked inside a Vincent of all faith and no voice.

Here, painting alone in a field among worms and corn, under a sky twisting with pale clouds, Vincent needed no words to convey God's words, each stroke of his brush a letter to Him. Praise God. It was words that had failed him, his failed words that had bred the mistrust of his congregation at the Borinage, where miners and their families regarded him with pity, his life even more wordless and impoverished than theirs. He was a lay preacher with two white shirts and no Latin, his head full of God but his plate empty— the miners' wives having to leave dishes of chickpeas and bacon scraps at his window lest he should starve. "Let his God take care of him," one miner said. "He is so in love with the Lord's goodness, let the Lord show some of it to him."

They wanted a real pastor, not the layman the mission had sent them, as if they were not deserving enough for an ordained priest, although they also knew that no priest wanted to come to them, to that cavern of coal, in that poverty without a tree, a shrub, or a single rose on the grilled landscape.

Vincent they got, a man burning with God and his message of God's burning love, which reached out to all, and especially to them, the lowest in man's eyes and therefore the highest in God's ken. By that view, Vincent would be at the pinnacle of the Lord's love, since he had nothing—a rented shack, a Bible, his few clothes— he had given away his only jacket and hat to an old man freezing and turning purple in a baker's doorway. He had given away his iron bed, too. And took to sleeping on the plank floor, on a nest he had devised from burlap sacks and newspapers.

"Look above at the stars and see God's alphabet in the heavens," he enjoined his small congregation one Sunday, reading from his notes, because he could not speak impromptu and he could not memorize his sermons. He seemed so far away from them, reading to them, his head a fiery nest nodding above the lectern. Few of them could read, let alone read the sky with its wondrous text. All the same, it was the holy words in the scriptures they wanted, and not the scrawls in the sky that only the redheaded man could decipher.

He was burning with God's word, burning with love, and, finally, just burning with fever, too ill to move, to speak, his eyes popping, a red fuzz of a beard on his sunken cheeks. It would have been better had he died right then, in his cold, makeshift bed and sooty sheets, and was dropped down an old coal shaft to save the burial expense, because it was worse than death to find, when he finally and miraculously recovered, a letter from the mission asking him to leave the Borinage and, indeed, to remove himself from all formal affiliation with their organization. He was a bootprint on the immaculate altar, spittle in the chalice. His religion was just fever; his life, not an example of Christ's self-sacrifice but of a madman hatless in the sun.

He stayed on after the expulsion, living off the little sums sent him by his father and brother, Theo. With all his time a great blank, he began to draw again, as he had when a child, and later, when, from his narrow English window, he limned the wet streets of Ramsgate, where he had been teaching, where daily he read the Bible, where he and God had found each other. Had he ever been out of God's sight? Never, of course, as nothing in the universe ever was.

But he had felt invisible to God, invisible, as well, to the pedestrians in the wet English streets, even when he stood there anchored, waiting for a sign, a jostle from the passing walkers to prove him alive. Later, in London, where he felt God's strongest pull (strongest at night, after he returned to his boardinghouse from a full day clerking in Goupil's art gallery), he read the Bible for comfort and instruction, and prayed to be visible in God's eyes. Pray as he might, there were still no signs for him. Only some while later when he rejoined his family in Holland did he think of following his father's priestly calling in order to merit visibility. To do good works for man and thus for God and His loving notice. More failure and invisibility.

Now he would pack up his paints, fold his easel, and return to his hotel and sip nothing but French beer and eat a bowl of leek soup with some slices of brown bread, then he'd climb to his attic room and wash his brushes carefully and cut some rags for the next day's cleaning and read a page or two from Shakespeare and drift off with the Englishman's words still in his head. In the early morning he'd start off to paint again—some blackbirds whirling in a thick field of living wheat ready to be mown or the Romanesque church tilting like a giant, golden muffin on the tilting hill.

But when he reached his hotel, he found a note waiting for him, an invitation to tea that very afternoon: "The cottage with the red path. For tea, at five," it said.

He many times had walked past that cottage with its wavy iron gate and red path on his way to the field beyond the Romanesque church, and once or twice had thought he had seen someone spying at him from behind the window curtain, eyes fixing themselves on him as he walked farther and farther out of sight. To be spied on, that, in itself, was unremarkable, since everywhere he went he was a stranger, and an oddity—an artist, and thus the subject of speculation—a grown man who did not go to regular work, and not a rich artist, either, of the kind known in the region. Like the landscapist Daubigny, for instance, who had owned his own house down the road and kept a lush garden and supported a family.

Vincent did not have a wife or a cat, did not have even a green branch stuck in a flower pot. And now he was being invited to tea. What French person drank tea at tea hour? When he worked at Goupil's in London, he learned, along with the whole city, to stop for tea, "Cupatai, hai?"

In the late, gray afternoon, a little amber furnace of tea to warm the formal day. And now, here, the furnace was being lit for him, but by whose hand? The invitation had come from no one he knew, since he knew no one but Dr. Gachet and his daughter, Marguerite, and the owner of his small hotel, Monsieur Ravoux, but the note had not come from them but from a "U," as the signature read. On heavy rag paper it was written, in a strong hand, the letters marching up and down little hills of a fine metal pen. "The cottage with the red path. For tea, at five."

He washed his gaunt face and patted down his hair with water. Crumbs of red earth and white paint still remained under his fingernails after brushing, and he thought of wearing the green gloves he had found under a slatted bench on the Seine a hundred or two years ago when he was still a shrimp in a bassinet, when he still thought love would come to him with a face like the North Sea. Blue eyes on a wild map. He made too much of such things then, fooling himself into hope. His own face the freckled belly of a poached, bearded salmon, his eyes, glass marbles that went blue in the shade.

He finally left the gloves in his traveling sack, carrying his own ungloved hands in his jacket. When he had walked as far as the Bad Café, he stopped to look at himself, feeling only partially clothed without his usual wardrobe of easel and paint box and camp stool. The tea enterprise, with its potential embarrassments, had further undressed him; what he needed was a strong calvados or marc to put a coat on his bare shoulders.

André did not dally and came right over, giving the bar top a few swipes of his towel—always a sign of favor, like a little pat on his client's shoulder. Today, for Monsieur Vincent, the first was a gift of the house. The proposal made things difficult, because if Vincent did not follow with buying another, it would seem he was being miserly and making profit on André's goodwill, and if Vincent refused, he would seem insulting, when no insult was warranted.

Vincent downed the calvados and quickly ordered a second, and soon after, a third. He realized it would take the three to get the coat on his naked shoulders and at least a half a bottle to see him fully attired; proper shoes might require an extra glass or two—and perhaps even another quick one to earn him a clean pair of suspenders. He was standing powerfully at the bar, André grinning a chummy grin, as when he wanted to engage you in conversation, wanted to know things, to get an edge on you, Vincent thought. Maybe to tell the police things, or make reports to officials from the hospitals and such places where they kept track on the doings of those they deemed mad and dangerous, disturbed people in general, anyone who did not own a house or show means of respectable employment, anyone with broken shoes.

"It must be good in your line of things, Monsieur Vincent," André said, half question, half assertion.

"Yes, not too bad," Vincent answered, feeling a blush of shame rise to his cheeks.

"Yes, I am sure, Monsieur Vincent, because every day for you is a holiday."

"Apropos," Vincent said frowning, as if recalling an important errand, "I have a little fête to attend," he said (his heart flopping about his tongue), "and I'm already late." Saying that with the intention of escaping further conversation (which would have ended by his painfully confessing that, indeed, he did not sell his paintings, had sold only one, and that his freedom and livelihood were earned for him), he remembered that, in fact, he did have a fête to attend, a tea with full silver service, room-high samovars the girth of steam engines, thimbles of spilling cream, and sandwiches with their brown edges cut away, the cups drowning with amber tea, a servant in a snail-shell cutaway standing by ready to replace whatever needed replacing.

The giant snail was asking him, "Monsieur Vincent, would you like another?"

There were so many snails like him at the hospital, putting their rubbery faces in his paint box and looking over his shoulder when he was painting. He, too, had wanted to be a snail but he was too red for snaildom. Red persons of either sex do not make good snails, the doctor had told him at his first hospital interview. "Their shells do not stay in place, slipping off them at the slightest emotion or breeze."

That diagnosis was a disappointment. To carry your house on your back and never to pay rent, that would be great; to have your house double as your coat, that would be as great; to move unhurriedly through time, eating, excreting, and reproducing while doing so, the whole organism self-sufficient and of hurt to no one—the happiness of the snail would never be his, the doctor assured him. Matter settled. Now on to the mineral baths in the lumbering tubs and the long afternoon rests and the quiet evenings surrounded by snails and some sad foxes. Turnips and undercooked whole eels in a wooden dish. Bars on the windows to keep the full moon from breaking in and, with its gravitational powers, suck, through the ears, the brain from its slippery moorings.

Paul had said to him that he was on a bad road. Paul, who was omniscient and who was always marching straight ahead on a well-paved road of his own paving. Paul knew everything about painting, past and present, knew everything about women, having been forever an anthropologist in their culture, and he knew, too, about how to move on when things got gloomy and how not to stay stuck in the sticky melting tar of Western civilization.

The painting surface should be flat, the color primal, the forms outlined to dispel any suggestion of illusionism; women with too much education drain the color of the unfinished paintings they come near, as in certain countries—and this was a known fact—menstruating women turn sweet milk sour. Western civilization was at its end, having already destroyed most other civilizations in its iron train; the artist, finally, is obliged to no one, to no principle, except to the higher call of his art, all other appeals—home, wife, children, the salvation of the world—all mere straws in the furnace.

He knew also that Vincent was more than half-way to drunkdom and that there was no person worse than a drunk who affected spirituality—humble and overblown in one. Vincent, in fact, for all his modesty and selfless efforts on behalf of other artists was raging with jealousy. He pretended to love other artists (the more mediocre the better), the better to conceal his envy. The little Dutch saint should just look after himself and leave others—and him, too—to fend for themselves. As for Vincent's paintings—some were not too dead. If Vincent would only conserve his energies, he might do good work in the future, but of course with the drinking, who could tell. Put less red in there.

Paul spoke so well, making everything true except the truth. It was his way to keep his shell strong, himself the very model of snail. Vincent could forgive him. Did, in fact, as he always would, knowing how strong Paul's art was and how Paul had only Paul to give himself strength. But he had God, Vincent did. (And Theo, of course!) Could a person want more?

"Yes, to be a good painter," Paul answered. Something that God had neglected to teach Vincent, having handed him out so many other marvelous favors.

They went back and forth like this in the morning over coffee and a slice or two of bread smeared with honey. Then they went off to work and smoked their pipes, painting in happy silence and liking each other until evening, when they recommenced their quarrels over a plate of rabbit stew in some café known for that specialty and known, too, for the wide credit it gave its regulars.

"How many rabbits have you eaten in your lifetime?" Paul asked.

"I have no idea."

"Say some number, two hundred, five hundred, a dozen?"

"Please, Paul, let's discuss something else. I have no wish to talk about rabbits."

"What of snails? Two thousand, five thousand, a dozen?"

Now Vincent could see the trick, Paul leading him into it, on a tight leash, like a blind dog to the pound.

"I never eat snails. I befriend them and love them," Vincent answered, watching Paul sprout buttery antennae from his head and his body capsize into his snail's calcified gray coat.

"Need nothing," Paul said, as he fled at snail's pace from the table and the café.

Paul stayed out that night, sleeping where? Under a cabbage leaf? At some brothel—at no charge—where he had endeared himself with stories of his childhood in Peru, raised in savage blood, singing under torture. Vincent stayed up reading, waiting, until four-thirty in the morning, then went to bed, having left a lamp lit in the hall for Paul to find his way in the dark.

In his sleep, he saw Paul's room below him and a troop of white asparagus growing out from the mattress of his friend's bed. Little and large stalks, some with thick shafts and rising like spears to pierce the ceiling and enter his room, others lying on their sides, sleeping, their tips resting on feathery pillows. Then it was morning and Paul returned only to pack and leave again. Vincent ventured into Paul's room, sure that the asparagus were still growing there, but found only a note filled with mundane instructions pinned to the pillow. Vincent was to post what little was left behind to Paul's address in Brittany. So long, good-bye.

Vincent had forgotten some few details of the event, Dr. Peyron told him one afternoon in the comfort of the doctor's paneled office at the asylum in Saint-Rémy, just the two, like gentlemen at their woody, carpeted club, over brandy and soda, while the halls and rooms just outside bulged with men and women cursing the walls and shuffling to the moon in their felt hospital slippers.

Paul and Vincent, the doctor continued, had parted after their meal at the café; Vincent went home, returning directly to the street with a razor gleaming in his hand. He spied Paul sauntering down the summer night and followed him, the trees' rustle covering his footsteps, until Paul, feeling someone at his back, turned about and found Vincent, crouching, razor above his head as if to slice the air and Paul's head along with it. Paul stared him down until Vincent finally uncoiled and slunk away to his hole in a corner of the upper house.

"Did Vincent remember that?" Dr. Peyron asked, in a kindly fashion.

"Not at all," Vincent answered, "because it never had happened." Perhaps Paul had imagined the story after he left Arles. It was a good story for Paul to tell, however; one in which he had mastered, by the power of his eye, an insane person ready to do him harm. Paul's vast knowledge extended to knowing how to subdue human beasts who tracked him in the streets, having learned in his youth to do such tricks on embittered lions in the Peruvian jungles.

Vincent did not tell the doctor about the room of gloating asparagus growing wildly after Paul had left in the morning, or of the army of snails parading on the walls in box formation that afternoon, or of the sadness that had bathed him ever since that day when Paul left, without a warm word. So long, good-bye.

But then, did Vincent remember going to a brothel, knocking at the door and presenting to one of its inmates—a young woman with a scarlet moon on her neck—a part of his ear wrapped in a bloody handkerchief?

Yes, he did recall that, and with shame and fear. For that act and for other reasons, he thought it best to rest a while and gather himself and his collapsed spirits, to stay here at the hospital in Saint-Rémy in the tender care of Dr. Peyron and others on the staff. And now that he was calm enough to paint, if only within the confines and borders of the hospital, he was certain that he was on the way to full repair.

"What was he thinking when he lifted the razor and carved out a bit of his ear?" Dr. Peyron asked, casually lighting his meerschaum as he spoke, wonderful clouds rising, as if from a baby locomotive buried in the pipe's wide bowl.

"Not of very much," Vincent answered. Actually, he had been remembering that he had left a box of very hard pencils in the field where he had been working the previous day with Paul. He could see the yellow box waiting there for him in a little fold of grass just as the blood ran down his neck. It did not hurt very much at the start.

Was he angry with someone when he did that act? Did he mean to cut himself elsewhere, on his neck, perhaps?

A boy had been looking at him all morning as he was painting in the courtyard garden, Vincent answered. Did the doctor know this boy?

He was not free to discuss his patients; of course, Vincent would appreciate that. He was called Vincent, but the man opposite was Dr. Peyron. He was Vincent, the man who had cut his ear and whose brother paid the bills. He painted. But he was out of harmony with his life, with a life that would bring him fullness and harmony. Perhaps one day, the doctor had promised, for he was still young, in his prime, in his great virile moment—what? thirty-seven?—he would marry and father children and manage an art gallery (as did his brother) or a business of some kind suited to his interest in art, and set aside a portion of his house—or even build a separate wing—in which he could retreat from the cares of the worldly week and devote the entire Sunday to his painting, to divert himself.

Yes, Vincent agreed, he would like that, a wife and children. Children were as good as paintings, better. Or just a wife, to start. A bride he would sit in the kitchen with and help cut the vegetables and slice the bread and shred the lettuce and put up the kettle. Live someplace in the country, a cottage with a thatched roof and lime-white walls, a stone fence covered with roses up to the gate's oak latch; an old, yellow Labrador with a rose stalk between his teeth sleeping in the garden path.

Then to paint every day and draw every hour and sketch even while sleeping with your bride beside you in the dawn. To make every day a painting Sunday. To live in God's grace, that is.

"And why did he not do so now?" the doctor asked.

"He lived in God's disgrace," he answered, feeling the shame come over him again, God's nothing.

In disgrace and shut away forever or for as long

as it was deemed unsafe for him out there, alone, worrying himself and hurting himself again.

Vincent painted. In the hospital corridors and vestibule, in his room, warming up to the paint as he glided and scrubbed it about, loving its wet aroma, the paint coming from the silvery tube like shoots of hot rain. They gave him back his pipe. He stewed in the wide earthern tubs, twice a day, two hours a day. Poached Vincent. Dry inside, filled with wheat husks and lentils, some barley in the ears. He needed sunshine and water, a whiff of the earth and its passionate chemistry. He was growing so calm now, couldn't he go outside for a little while and paint or just do some drawing and sketches, a little notation on the page, to let God know, you know, that Vincent hadn't forgotten God's outside while he, Vincent, was locked inside?

Yes, he was mending, and in the early spring he was allowed to paint in the asylum's enclosed park—the trees like skimpy stage props wishing to come alive, some strolling patients, for the sake of the blue, a solitary figure walking into a hedge, himself that is, doing what he had always done.

He was healing the slow way that would take him a few more lifetimes if he remained in the asylum, and perhaps he was not healing at all, wanting to lie with a woman but finding his moldy blanket in her place, wanting a woman's affectionate word sometime in the day or in the morning when he dressed in the dark. One afternoon, for real nourishment, he ate some paint squeezed from the silvery tubes, and a week later, he tried to wash it all down with kerosene drawn from a lamp. He could consume such poisonous fare anywhere, even outside the hospital's walls, so why pay to stay where he felt more and more a convict with an undetermined sentence?

Theo petitioned for Vincent's freedom. "We will release him," Dr. Peyron replied, "but only in the care of a professional or responsible person; your brother should live in a calming place, which, in my opinion, excludes Paris for the moment."

Vincent had wished the old painter Pissarro would take him in—room and board to be paid for by Theo, naturally. Who would not have wished Pissarro for a father-friend? Everyone envied the patriarch's children, who were allowed to draw and paint and scribble the hours away under the open sky while others their age were kept pressed to their schoolbooks and shunted off to gloomy places.

Pissarro liked Vincent, esteemed the Dutchman's extravagant paintings, and perhaps at another time Pissarro would have lodged him in the warm heart of his large family and strolled with him and taken meals with him and soothed him when the Dutchman's jagged nerves began to wear through to his skin. But a man who could cut off his own ear could, just as readily, when the mood ravished him, lop off the ear of another, Pissarro's own lovely daughter's, say.

Not to Pissarro, then, but straight from the asylum in Saint-Rémy to the riverside village of Auvers-sur-Oise, twenty miles from Paris, and to the protection of Dr. Paul Gachet, friend of artists and himself an artist, Vincent reluctantly went.

"Paul. Yes, you must at once call me Paul," Dr. Gachet said.

Tired from his journey, fatigued from his climb up the hill from the narrow train depot to Gachet's house, Vincent had expected—and had wished for—a greeting more reserved than the doctor's agitated hand-pumping and his fraternal embrace, the clinging hug of one drifting soul searching for the anchor of another. Vincent felt the familiar strain of disappointment come over him, draining away the shallow well of his hope. So, too, Vincent's language drained itself of color.

"Well, here I am, arrived, finally," Vincent said, the huge parcel of his belongings still at his feet where he had dropped it on the doctor's affectionate pounce.

Pipe smokers, the two sat in a cloud of burning tobacco. Tired from his journey and anxious to find a place to stay and get settled, Vincent sat politely while the doctor unburdened himself.

It was the best that could have happened to Vincent, coming to him, because he knew they would be great friends and help each other's art, and take away some of the loneliness, too, because in spite of his active medical practice and his own etching and painting and cooking up herbal concoctions for his patients—free of charge, he might add—to allow the body, by the stimulation of his herbs, to cure itself with its own healing juices, he was lonely.

There was no question that Vincent would recover, now that he was out—if you would forgive his saying—of the madhouse, where all those ill people about him were sure to keep him ill and even make him sicker.

"The sane cannot make the ill well, but the insane can make the well sick," Gachet said, circling his pipe stem about his ear. Then, realizing the gesture might be taken to suggest Vincent's escapade with his ear, the doctor rose and extended his arms. "No, no, not you, my dear Vincent, health shall rise in you with a great flow, a great flowering."

The doctor's furniture began to make Vincent dizzy. In a room so airy and light, where the windows opened to the trees and the wonderful aromas of the garden, hyacinths and rosemary and all the various herbal stuffs that went from the flowering garden into the square green bottles of the doctor's healing medications, the black furniture took the air from his lungs, leaving him in airless darkness. Giant toadstools and wild mushrooms rose above the trees to block out the light and air from heaven. He would rise and walk away before the mushrooms umbrellaed the earth with their leathery brown canopies, but he was caught there by the doctor's goodwill and hunger to please, to be loved.

In that, Dr. Paul Gachet was his more famished brother. But Vincent thought he had his own hunger better managed, pretending to have eaten at all hours of the day and night, needing nothing—a drop of water for company's sake—while, in truth, loneliness was his tapeworm and true companion.

Vincent dragged himself out the door of the Bad Café, leaving behind a significant tip, just to show who was who, though André, in a show of pride—one does not tip the *patron,* he whispered—refused to accept it, leaving the coins glowing on the zinc counter to stay there, he declared, until whenever Vincent chose to return or until crows went early to confession.

He took the road slowly. What time was it? Surely too late for tea. What a relief, now he'd return to his room and send off a note of apology: Got drunk at the Bad Café while waiting for boots to be repaired. The heels worn down to a slope, the uppers cracked and crusty, old bread loaves left in the sun. The town hall clock said five, exactly, and it would be five down the road at the cottage, too, the hot water just at a boil, the kettle steaming in the kitchen while the ladies pried the hot biscuits from their pans.

He had missed nothing and would have to find excuses all over again for not coming. No, he would have to eat his dread and present the salmon of himself whole. Past the town hall and up and down roadways and walled houses to the cottage itself, the twisting red path leading to it, the iron gate topped with wavy spear tips, the lush green garden.

Now he was at the door. A red cat with a gray string dangling between its teeth eyed him before crashing through the reeds. It was quiet inside the door, no rattling of silver, no teaspoons banging in the cups, no voices in the parlor; he was ready to leave, having entered the wrong house at the wrong hour of the wrong day.

"Please do come in, Monsieur Vincent," a young woman's voice called from a room within.

Chapter 6

And within that room, on a blazing white divan, a young woman, her hair on fire, was sleepily pouring tea. Vincent recognized the boy in the fields and the boy in the asylum now in a woman's white pinafore and a black ribbon about her white throat.

"That was Jack he had seen," she said, answering him. No, not *Jacques,* the way the French say it, but *Jack*, and should they ever become friends and wish to remain friends he would always have to call her Jack, in the proper British way, because when she was attired as a young man, it was a British, and not a French, lad she had become.

Vincent agreed, but as she was now not Jack, who was she, and finally, he asked shyly, his heart doing tricky things, who was she to him? A piece of scone broke from his mouth, crumbling into his lap. She was Ursula, she said, giving him a second napkin, one so thick he could have painted on it—an admirer.

How weak that word, she said immediately, so reeking of the salon and its affectation and insincerities, of everything she hated. While it was his art that she respected because it was everything the salon was not.

Vincent looked about him, at the book-lined room, the dense green carpets, the French windows giving out to a ripe green garden, the stillness itself an object of furniture like the highboy laden with thick toast still steaming from the oven, blue pots of jams, marmalade and quince, little wooden tubs of yellow butter beading in the June heat.

Ursula rested her cup on a stack of books mounting beside her: *À Rebours, Fleurs du Mal, Leaves of Grass, Studies in the Renaissance, Sister Agatha's Ordeal,* the rest blocked from view by her curtaining skirt.

And where did she see his paintings, since only few had ever seen them, unless she had visited his brother's gallery in Paris, but how would she have known about their being there, in any case? He could feel himself sweating, because he did not want to ask anything or say anything at all, because he wanted to go up to her and lick her neck, undo the ribbon about it and the rest of anything covering her shoulders and arms.

"Because of the tea," he said, the heat and the tea and the closed room, the tea especially pumping his heart the faster and making him perspire. "Think nothing of it." Did he say that, think nothing of it? He had meant that she should think everything of it, that she should understand his salty sweat was love's chemistry stewing him in his own Dutch sauce.

Did he require another napkin? she asked, because she had bins of them.

"Save them for the other guests," Vincent said.

There were, of course, no other guests, whatever had given him that idea, and why in the world would he want others, when he was, as was she, ever and mostly alone.

He stopped sweating, having come to the perfect cooked moment. Now he could serve himself up.

And she, was she an artist? he asked, looking about the room again for evidence of her work, looking about to keep himself from staring at her.

It was the new art, if he would grant her that, photography she was concerned with—one day she'd show him her prints of leaves and stems taken in her garden, right out there, over her shoulder, she said, her eyes half shutting, her body softening.

Was she sleepy? Vincent asked, feeling he had already bored her with the dull evidence of himself. Not sleepy at all, though she had taken something to calm her just before he arrived, to calm herself for his arrival, in fact.

To be calm for the two of them, knowing how disquieted he was generally, how he was, forgive her for saying, always trembling. Even if his body did not noticeably rattle, it was quivering, as when she first saw him in the hallway, in the midst of all the sluggish hospital traffic, sitting there on his wooden stool, before his easel, torturing paint on the canvas.

He was rough looking with his plain worker's clothes, a road mender or stone cutter with thick-soled lace-up boots and a coarse white cotton blouse buttoned to his adam's apple, his trousers iron gray, baggy, and spotted with paint flecks, and he wore an iron-gray vest, a pipe in the chest pocket, the rim charred and ancient. His head was always shaking, nodding, as if agreeing with an invisible speaker, his eyes burning and red. He had tried to kill himself; she had heard the hospital talk.

To kill herself, she well understood that, to get rid of herself, but slowly and calmly and with soft ease, sleeping herself away to oblivion—to leave the embrace of Somnus for the bed of his brother, Death—by extending sleep—a nap to a siesta to a slumber, etcetera—longer and longer each day until the sleep of the day and the sleep of the night converged and crossed over sleep's soft bridge to an easeful end. But this man, she had heard, went about it violently, cutting off a part of his ear. How much of himself and for how long could he go on carving away before *he* was carved away?

(Better he murder the world than slice himself. Not kill animals, though, except, perhaps, the human ones who hunted foxes, say, their charming, foxy hearts pounding to burst as the hounds and humans chased them in open field and ravine.)

Yes, that was when she first saw him, in the hospital. One day, positioning herself behind a pillar, she watched him set up his easel in the courtyard garden. She could see the painting itself, a painting depicting the very courtyard in which he sat: the stone well in the center, the leafy wild shrubs along the court's margin, and the ocher walls and green door leading into the hospital's depths. His painting showed all the garden's essential features, the shrubs and plants, the well fringed with lilacs, but he had twisted them extravagantly, beyond the boundaries of human sense.

Still, his painting looked to her like the garden, and the garden like the painting. The painting was alive, but it was the weird offspring of a crazy father, who himself resembled a large child with a paint box. She had wanted to laugh at the trembling, lunatic colors, at the trembling canvas, looking as if it would sail off the easel and, like a postage stamp, stick itself to a cloud.

She herself sailed off from the hospital not too long after seeing him, taking with her the image of the trembling man. Although the violence of the act against himself had troubled her, she respected him for trying to kill himself so obliquely, taking a piece of himself for the whole, a synecdoche of suicide, she said to a woman on the boat from Calais to London. The woman,

Zoella, her lover and sometime friend. She liked, too, that his painting resembled nothing before born from a thoughtful human's hand, showing a mind extravagant, wandering outside the pale to places where the divine revealed itself through and behind what was seen.

She herself had tried so hard to locate those places with her photographs—her failures, her ruins and farces. Not to hunt out God in a scramble of waving hills and hay and charging clouds or funereal cypress trees that shivered blackly under a night of stars—images that jumped from the quivering man's paintings the orderlies had stacked outside his door while the room was being cleaned and inspected and their maker was up to his neck in an earthern tub—that was not her business. But she recognized the impulse, herself longing not merely to capture what was before her camera by way of recording vistas and places exotic and otherwise, or the portraits of personages great and ordinary—but, with her lens, to imprint—as she noted in her diary—the structure of beauty.

She herself was a structure of beauty, her lover of the moment had told her. She was so young, her body so perfect, such breasts proved God's existence (and that He was a woman), her aroma, a stand of wild jasmines on a nighttime summer hill in Tangier or Fez, and so forth. It was normal for her to have such transcendental ambitions, all young people did, especially when they were exquisitely sensitive as she was, and as demanding of perfection and of the original—all creations of a type, all persons of a type being mere failures and cheats, belonging to the world of the less.

The impatience of the young, the arrogance of the young, the unforgivingness of the young, the perfectionism of the young, the judging everyone as lacking and inferior, were not these the causes of her unhappiness (and the very source of her appeal), her lover asked, as the train approached the lobster shell of Paris. They were on their way to a holiday in London, Ursula now cured of sadness forever through the ministrations of the doctors in Saint-Rémy.

She had gone there for a fit of nerves that had lasted too long, looking for her papa under dinner plate and Moroccan carpet, crying for him over soup while her two young Parisian friends and Zoella worried over her. He had died, that papa. He who was once never there, now could never be there, even if ever he had desired it. Yet his legacy, if not he, in person, always stood beside her. Because of him she had never to work or to be concerned about money, for whatever there was of it, it was always enough for her photographic equipment, for her travel, for her cozy cottage and garden, for clothes of both sexes, for sitting at André's café, drinking and smoking there until eleven o'clock or 'til midnight, if she wished, and enough, especially, for the morphine—for that was the calming stuff she had taken before his coming—and all the needles to transfer it into her sleepy body, keeping it drowsy and calm.

A pride of lions, a den of foxes, a fit of nerves. It was the latter, prompted by her father's death and all the morphine she had taken to soothe the pain of that death that had sent her for the cure in Saint-Rémy, where educated and artistic loons mixed with loons of ordinary plumage—bakers gone mad from oven's heat and the yet greater sorrows of flaming bread and impotent yeast, trainmen turned crazy counting ties and missing stations in the night. "And clockmakers, too," she said, "throwing clocks out of windows to see time smash." "A hospital joke," Ursula added, "the doctors loved repeating." Her father had died and she came to grief and wanted to be Jack forever, Ursula, at eighteen, having died with her father, going up in smoke with him in the same chimney.

Her ashes fell down to earth at the hospital in Saint-Rémy, landing in a wide bed where the doctors let them cool and reform themselves— sunshine, calm, soothing words and steady broth—Vincent knew the regime, of course.

(I came to learn this and more, across the later reaches and walls dividing time, when windows flamed along the avenues and we slept away the afternoons and talked all the cooling morning, in the first intense days of her visit, when nothing was left out, not even our dreams fresh from the dreaming, when the world had winnowed down just to us, all other music fallen silent at the bed's edge.)

If not a structure of beauty, she was stunning to those who first set eyes on her and even later, after you saw her many times and you would think you would be used to her special quality or that it would have worn away, as beauty does, after repeated viewing, you were still stunned, especially if you turned a corner and she was there, a child sitting in her father's garden and making, all by herself, quietly and without mother, friends, or governess, a wreath of grass and windflowers to crown her loneliness.

Her father woke one day when she was nine and thought he had struck his head against the bedpost, but the blow came from seeing her, as everyone else with living eyes had been seeing her, as beautiful.

Ravishing is more the word. For without wishing it, she brought to those who spied or viewed her the feeling of being flooded with a joy of longing and deprivation. It was what her father felt that morning he woke and supposed he had cracked his head on the stone lintel of his bedroom door.

He did not see stars; he saw hundreds of floating and spinning cameos of his daughter, cameos that went directly into his bloodstream and imprinted themselves into his cells. That is how he explained to his closest friend why he had to send her far away from him. Even at that, far away was not far enough, since she was now in his cells and lived with him and was part of every other thought, even when he was in his kitchen cooking a flayed and gutted rabbit in wine sauce.

His daughter's enchanting image did not make him want to dive into the well, nor did he think of ways of seducing her soul, as would have certain fathers. He thought to stow himself away, so that whenever he was in his daughter's presence, he would become invisible. A better plan came some hours later after he returned from the café and drinking its deranging beverages: He would make his daughter, not himself, invisible, so that her person would in no way pertain to his presence or thought, and thus she would not—or he would not—leave a window open to depravation.

To England she went, not understanding why she was being sent, for none of her father's explanations—the joy of her learning new things in a new country, whose useful language she would rapidly master—had satisfied her. She left Auvers-sur-Oise, left France, feeling dark shame, believing that she had done something wrong, something indicating and confirming to the world her true, wrong nature.

Odd, in any case, to the English girls and the teachers of her new home and school. She already spoke English well enough, so there was no cause on that part for her to feel estranged, but she did not like the low seriousness of the others, they did not willingly read poetry or look up at the sky and imagine pirate corsairs running through high swells, leaving ports ruined, in flames and cursing God.

By sixteen, without any show of power and without any interest in doing so, her presence quietly infused the school. The students loved her and those who hated her loved her; the teachers adored her—one actually suffering distractions through the spring term, dreading in advance the summer, which would take Ursula away to Swiss holidays. One companion Ursula's age returned home before midyear to London, her parents taking her away in a cool breeze.

"Ursula, never forget me," she cried.

Ursula waved her off then returned to Tennyson weeping over the death of his young friend, the poem far sadder than the departure she had just witnessed.

Experience itself is nothing, she thought to herself, just raw earth. Only experience transmuted by the imagination gives significance to the experience. She wrote that in her journal, meant for, and scattered with, such observations.

Not that she was indifferent to experience, but that was Jack's business. Jack, who prowled the night, hands in jacket pockets, shoulders hunched, with the rolling walk of a common sailor. Jack, in search of opium dens in alleys off quays (she never found one, but was sold a good-luck amber bead by a sailor just returned from China), Jack combing prostitute streets where Ursula dared not step, Jack burning at all hours with a hard, gemlike flame. Jack be nimble. Not the fruit of experience, but the living thing itself, every day and every hour, febrile, feverish, burning with life. Jack be quick.

"Yes, well, one day," Vincent said, "perhaps she would show him her photographs," one day when she was less sleepy, less falling into the tea service.

Perhaps, when she knew him better, though that may never happen because she knew him better enough, knew all she would ever know or need to know of him and the iron weave he was made of. Incidentally, would he help her now by leaving?—because there was so much emotion in seeing him that she was drained from the emotion of seeing him.

She rose, unsteadily, and Vincent went up to take her arm and lead her out into the garden for the air, to let nature revive and invigorate her. They walked in circles under a reddish full moon—would it shower tomorrow?—a cat prowled underfoot then dashed savagely away in the foliage.

And he, Monsieur Vincent, was he not overtaken by this meeting? she asked, though he need not answer immediately; he could let her know by post, or better, he could set a fire in one of his fields and signal her by smoke, as the Apache Indians did one another when they went to war.

He would answer her right away, Vincent said, to save money on the post and to spare the world some matches and straw. "Wait," she said, "let me lie down here and catch" ("Catch what?" Vincent asked) "my wind," and down she went, softly, into a patch of moss and wild succulents, so that but for moonlight and her white dress, Vincent would scarcely see her.

"Yes," she said, "you may begin."

He began with difficulty. Speaking his feelings was the difficulty, he said, not that he did not care for words, value them, even; in writing, the words flowed easily, because he was not entirely himself but also the pen and the ink and there was no auditor to judge him face-to-face as he milked the words from his feelings and to make him hesitate with each phrase, some words strangling in the windpipe, others waylaid in the throat, the rest, who had survived, coming out wounded, as from a cave of ambushes.

He had tried, once, to tell people about God and His interesting love for them but he had failed, his words murdered before they saw light. So, would she then understand how, in this unusual case of theirs, the difficulty was all the greater, his own words hiding from him at their birth.

"Find them soon," Ursula said, her voice falling far away into her and trailing into the leaves.

"Beware of love . . ." Vincent began.

"Love?" Ursula asked, raising her head from the grass.

"*Liefde op 't eerste gezicht,* love at first sight, I mean. An artist friend told me that long ago when I was looking at paintings in his studio.

Beware of it, of such love, the one that strikes down like lightning, flames everywhere in the head. Of paintings he was speaking. The one you like the first and quickest, standing there in the middle of the studio or gallery is not always the one you will like the best later, after you have gotten over the lightning bolt, the flames burned out."

"Do you think I'm still in flames, Vincent?"

"I was speaking of mine," Vincent said, laughing. "Once, I was in love, in Holland, and I promised to keep my young hand in a candle flame for as long as the woman I loved would let me speak of it to her. Because she did not love me and did not wish me speak of my love for her. I did not keep my hand in the flame because her family made me stop, but I blistered anyway, and some skin fell off. Almost charred, you see."

"Glorious!" Ursula exclaimed. "I knew you were capable of that and more. Yes, and even more."

"When I first saw you," Vincent continued, "the lightning used me as its tallest tree, and I was burned up in an instant. But I soon grew back whole, trunk and branches and roots, and with a cold eye for you, and I admired you more than when I saw you through love's flames. So, I loved you at first sight and at second sight."

"Didn't I suppose this?" Ursula asked herself.

"And, as you were speaking, I wondered whether I would put my hand in fire for you, as

I once did for that good woman made of sensible kitchen soap."

"And your answer?"

Vincent lay himself down beside her on the leaves and cold earth, his voice at first a whisper, then lowering further as she took his hand and led him, with encouraging sighs, into the glade of sleep.

He often remembered that afternoon and the evening in the garden, sometimes even when he was painting or writing a letter. That had been a good sleep, the moon tilted above his eyes, the red cat, returned from his hunt, nestling himself beside Ursula, warming himself in the flames of her hair.

Remembered that evening when, weeks later, they climbed the hills of the Buttes-Chaumont on their Paris holiday, reaching the Corinthian temple at the park's highest point, the city stretching out beyond them to the edge of the civilized world. Some children with their young parents stood solemnly viewing the prospect. Ursula thought them from the provinces; Vincent said they had come from the poorer sections of Paris, the man's oiled boots and recently brushed gray vest told him that—a stone breaker, a road mender with his family, come all this way from Montparnasse for a day's outing, a dark beer or two in one of the park's café terraces, a pony ride and sherbet for the little ones. The wife was very proud of her man and he of her and they of their children. Vincent beamed in their presence, the worker and his holy family.

Paul once advised him to have children. "Without them, Vincent, you will go into the winter of your life," he said. Paul was always in the spring of his, having long ago left his wife and children to live in tropical sunshine with a fifteen-year-old Tahitian who modeled and kept house for him—all so far away, the jungle rushing its green life up to Paul's open window.

Ursula pointed to the white plaster cake of the Sacré-Coeur, the church sitting on the hill of Montmartre. "The French army slaughtered the Communards in those hills," she said. "Women and children, too. Three thousand, Vincent, many with bayonets."

"There goes an honest family," Vincent said, knowing that she had just spoken but, in his concentration on the four who went by, descending a path to the base of the park, not heeding what she had said. "The kind at the heart of God's favor."

"Oh! I forgot you know so much about God." The chill in her voice woke him. "Yes," he confessed, "that did sound pious." Would she forgive him the piety, yet welcome the sentiment?

Did he suppose his homilies would win her over to the side of the bourgeois family? To join the class that had murdered the workers on these very hills? He did not know her at all then, not an iota of her. She'd go back to women before she'd have children—and she might go back anyway. To have herself tortured by that bourgeois arrangement, she'd kill herself first, and not slowly, either, like some weaklings she knew, drowning themselves in beer suds and apple juice.

"That is a good idea, a drink," Vincent said. (To uncurdle his blood, he thought.) What did she think of that?

"Finally, Monsieur, you have recognized that I am here."

"Always here," Vincent said, touching his chest Arab fashion. Yes, a drink or three would do her well, but not before a little exercise, a ride about the fantastical grounds, its fabricated mountains and manmade lake, fed by streams gushing from manmade caves, the whole park the artifice of artisans and engineers, of nature bettered. Imagine what the century to come would accomplish!

Once below, Ursula paused at a flower stall, buying a single iris, her present to Vincent. He searched about for a flower to exchange for hers, but she objected; his would not be a spontaneous gesture but an act of trade—suitable for a tradesman, but he was an artist, was he not?

Ursula hired a pony cart for the hour. But hardly had they gone a few hundred feet, she reined in at a clearing and took Vincent's hand. "No more speaking," she said, "for as long as we can bear it, and until only something poignant is said."

There they sat, in the wicker cart, Vincent

clutching his iris, Ursula perusing her book of Whitman's poems, the pony courting the motes in the day, until an hour had passed, when they paid the hire and walked, hand in hand, silently, all the way to their little hotel on the Quai Voltaire.

Exhausted from their walk, they jumped to bed with their clothes on, lying beside each other, face-to-face for long minutes. Vincent threw his boots to the floor; Ursula slid off her thin shoes, a whisper of paper hitting wood. Someone whistled frantically in the street below. Life crackled in the walls.

"Who will speak first?" Ursula asked.

"I shall," Vincent said, "to continue what I began to say that night in your garden, when sleep filled your ears."

"You," she said, "your voice was so low that it put me to sleep."

"Perhaps I have somnific powers that I could bring to medicinal use."

"The hand in the flame," Ursula reminded him.

"No, not my hand, except to save your life, and then I would shroud myself in fire if needed. No, I thought more of how I would live with you and by you, however your mood shifts and disposition alters, whatever mean shafts you mine to bring disintegrations to our table and darkness to our bed.

"The smallest part of you that stays wholesome is all I ask. All the rest of what is you, of whatever grows corrupt or malignant in you, is just bad weather passing. As long as there is a healthy cell left in you, I'll love you and I'll stay."

"Did you speak with such fervor to your congregation, Vincent?" Ursula asked.

"I tried."

"And with such grace?"

"Inconceivable."

"Perhaps one day you might approach some congregation again, Vincent, for there is no lack in your speech now. I do not know what God might still find wanting in your words, but whatever inch of reserve in me there was left to win, you have won," she said.

Chapter 7

He was still there, in the Bad Café, the glass of absinthe in his hand, that freckled red paw, too gross, too untrustworthy for her love. He had betrayed her by leaving his watch, by allowing his impatience to take him from his sworn post by her bed. And he was now drunk, besides—a cheerless, blood-drained drunk, his body weighted, his boots iron-shod, his head a baby anvil—a splendid model of sobriety for Ursula.

He finally lifted himself out of the chair and went from the café, leaving the door ajar behind him and the sleeping smudges (now become owls and crows) at their tables, and he made his exhausted way—a little stumble, a little trip over his boots, a few lurches into the nettle bush by the road—until he was almost there, *chez* Ursula. The moon above him was more loony than ever, now that it was hardly there in the sky at all, a little faint wafer in the dawn. He was almost there, *chez* Ursula, the sleeping princess, the red fire, the red waif with red sex. The wafer moon was disappearing but the true moon was hanging on an old tarred rope above her cottage, above her sleeping tower and chamber of dreams.

Vincent would invade her dreams, step into their vague stage, rewrite her script and gloomy part, and fashion players and scenes cast to his vision for her happiness. Gone the old haunting misery clinging to her day life, and in a shot—presto!—all her sadness transformed to joy.

For all the salubrious thoughts of stages and altered scripts, Vincent was apprehensive. He had left his post and there was a price to pay, unless she was still sleeping and unaware of his desertion, his infidelity to his word, which sent her into morose caves and trembling like a child lost in a vast cavern. But, finally, he knew his conduct did not dictate what she would do or how she would show herself to him, Ursula always offering up a tray of surprises.

One tender day in the field near the Romanesque church, she read a novel on a blanket beside him while he painted away the hours. They stayed the whole day in telepathic happiness, returning to her cottage in a night bulging with stars and flying moons. They sat in the kitchen at the old pine table covered with pâtés in crocks and tubs of butter and sweet pickles and two loaves of dark bread. They drank Norman cider from the bottle. They let the candles die.

He woke that morning alone. It felt like noon, the cider a thief of hours, but it was only dawn. She was gone from the bed at an hour she usually would be anchored in it. He first searched in the kitchen, then in all the rooms of the house, where nothing hinted of her. He went through the garden and stood some feet from the outhouse, taken by a strange gasping and humming from inside. He called out and received no answer. He knocked at the door and still had no reply. Alarmed that she was ill, he opened the door, finding her there naked on the commode, a syringe at her feet, each rose nipple pierced by a fine sewing needle.

She looked up at him without seeing him or the light and the space of the day.

"Just shit, just shit," she whispered.

Now he silently entered the cottage and crept his way to the bedroom. What would he do now, when her bed was again empty, the cottage empty and silent everywhere? He dared not investigate the garden and its little shed. In the kitchen, some large sheets of paper tacked to the pine table spoke for her.

She was leaving, for a while. But she was going from him forever. She was going to Paris. And should he think this was a mere whim, let him consider her handwriting, the visual proof of the force of her decision to leave him. (Note, he could hear her say, the upward fleck of her "t's" slashed high on the page, and observe the deep impress of her pen—evidence all more telling than the words themselves.)

While she was absent, would he consider how he could explain himself, make himself known to her—through the post, as he was so fond of writing letters—without guise, without defenses, pure, his heart laid bare, to paraphrase a French poet she admired. (She would admire him, thought Vincent, and his gray city flowers born in smelly darkness and rot, the sickly spawns of gutters and sewers.) Perhaps, one day, with the proper explanations for his misbehavior, she would hope to forgive him his betrayals.

Perhaps he also would be forgiven his trying to stop her from sticking in her long, golden thigh the needle filled with the stuff that took sadness away and which pricked her youth away as well; forgive his trying to stop her from disappearing, when the mood struck, to Paris, with its iron needle sticking into the sky of her very young life.

Now, he thought, he would take his time waiting for her forgiveness, that he would let her go, because there was no reasoning with her, her moods and wishes quicker than a spilled bowl of mercury hurtling along a madhouse corridor or spilling down the table's edge in great globs only to climb as silvery beads to the tips of trees, reflecting there, among the leaves and branches, fractured, glistening images of sky and clouds.

And, the letter continued, until he came to be just and measured, she would insult him as she wished and leave him when she wished. He had no authority over her, no rights to her. No, Monsieur Vincent had none, not to her person, not to her thoughts, not to her wishes, because he was

nothing but a little impotent nothing—a Dutchman with his canals drained and sluices clogged.
A madman, officially. And perhaps he was not
even so interesting or good at that, his madness
just fits of nerves and disgusting alcohol, just a
little case of human incapacity, hardly more than
a pathetic instance of self-pity.

No, not so much a real madman as a real *homme
raté*—a failure in everything: in his art, just shit;
in bed, fit only to make her green with seasick-
ness; nothing, too, were his lofty ideas—the
goodness of life and the sweetness of God—mere
fancies of a powerless man, the justifications of a
giant failure, him.

Vincent could find his way to agree to all that.
He had thought it all before, believing it all
about himself, all but his belief in the goodness
of life and of God, for that was a truth outside of
himself, not a truth born of his failure. For all its
sorrow, the world was good, and so too its mysterious creator. Even at its worst, even in the
deepest coal mine, the sooty skin of coal dust on
your blackened faced, the fine black dust sweating the lungs and heart, even there, in that dark
shaft, God was sending you His infusing sunny
rays to brighten your soul. Praise God for the
miracle of life, the window of His unfolding universe.

To Paris now she would go, to spend nights
among her kind, among the women who adored
her and to lie with Morpheus, who let her forget
pain as long as she praised him by melting his

drowsy plasma into her tissue and blood, she being at once the host of forgetfulness and the very thing forgotten.

Now she was going to Paris, to the chief den and capital of her God, where she'd spend days in that hotel for women like herself, spending how many days and nights in that private salon of potted plants and thick mocha carpets, that darkened room, as she had once described it, strewn with half-dressed, languid women, its walls crowded with fashionable paintings—a Puvis de Chavannes Arcadia of youths and maidens in blue and rose robes in a pale olive grove by a flat Aegean bay—the room where she sped morphine into her creamy thighs.

The thighs he loved as with everything of her he loved. Besotted, the British would say. A calf in love, a Dutchman drunk with love, from the first sip of the first sight—the lightning bolt, the *coup de foudre,* into his brain into his heart into his cock and balls, straight down to his big toe. One day a scientist would discover the chemistry of passion, explaining, once and for all, how, in the beloved's presence, the brain issues its recipe to cook certain juices in the blood, which sends the heart and lungs and all other toiling organs a mysterious and lunatic hunger. The mind is the last to know.

"Vincent, you have no measure," she once said. "Look at me and how proportionately I love you. Give yourself some measure." She, however, was all proportion. Her body just the right fit for her little cottage, for her studio which held so compactly and neatly the bulky equipment of her art. Her teas, never too much or too little of anything, just enough of the little white cakes and cucumber sandwiches (though Vincent gulped down pawsful of them and still was hungry); even the copper kettle on the stove did not whistle too extravagantly, nor did its plume of steam describe strange arcs or animal forms—a six-humped camel or a wolf with a rose between its teeth, or forms suggestive of blurry sexual organs decomposing in space.

Everything about her and hers, except for Vincent, was balanced. So, too, was her lovemaking: delicate and sweet and subtly animal in unpredictable turn—didn't he agree? Their lovemaking: He was used to brothel ways and their time economies; she lasted longer with women, but, then, with women, she savored it more, as she did the pages of an erotic novel before falling asleep. She would turn to sleep with a whisper of his name, while he continued to feed her ear with sighs of love.

Trembling, as always, that Vincent, his body shuddering long after lovemaking, shuddering for her, for all the lost years he did not know her and therefore had missed her, for all the years his body was mute and flat from want of love's touch, and for all the eternity he'd spend without her in a grave with busy vermin for company. Of course, he exaggerated. As he did with everything, she'd point out. His unnatural longing for her was just an ax to keep her frightened, and thus to keep her thinking of him *sans cesse*—though, she had to admit, she liked the sensation of imagining his freckled red hatchet poised over her head.

Enough of ruminations! (When, in the few hours he was gone, did she have all the time to write this endless letter, Vincent wondered?) She was off to catch the early train to Paris, while he, of course, still would be sleeping with a broken plough in a ditch or he'd be in his stuffy crib of a room snoring loudly enough to deafen the flies. But before she took the train for Paris, she would, and for reasons unknown even to herself, give him one last chance to apologize, and to demonstrate by that act, his capacity, as brutish as it may be, for unselfish kindness—the sort he had shown to fallen caterpillars he gingerly returned to their leaf.

This charity on her part should be seen as an instance of her general balance and proportion—as cited earlier in the letter. Although it was not her place to do so, she would have swallowed her pride and even searched for him at the Bad Café, where he undoubtedly had slunk away while she was sleeping, but as he knew, she was banned from there, temporarily, even though in her heart she had forgiven them all, even André, the meanest—and, actually, the most charming—of them all.

She had gone to the café one afternoon in her boy's outfit, complete with peaked cap. They were used to that. Even to having to call her Jack, a name no one could correctly pronounce in the English manner, as she had insisted they do. But this time, and against all of Vincent's admonitions and his attempts to block her way at the cottage door, she went there with a bulky revolver stuck in the belt of her trousers. She was going to wait and show them up for the cowards they were, sitting there at the rear of the Bad Café with a milky absinthe in hand and her pistol on the table, and wait for any hint of a jibe directed at her or at any deliberate mispronouncing of her name or any jokes about her standing to take a leak.

The regulars were all there: Salvatore, Pissy Marie, and Louis, with his famous red bulb of a nose, but those three had been respectful of her—of "him," especially Louis.

And the mockers and insulters were there, too, giving her a sardonic grin of recognition. André nodded as she entered and took her order without a word and delivered the drink to the table, giving it a single, exaggerated swipe of his bar towel. Jack pulled the revolver from under her belt and casually dumped it on the table. She looked about her to note the effect of the revolver's thud, her eyes set hard against all comers.

Louis rose from his drink and came over to say some friendly words about the weather, and Pissy Marie smiled a toothy hello. Her Salvatore gave Jack a philosophical shrug, as if to indicate that he didn't know any more about life than he had an hour ago or maybe he was asking, by that lifting of his shoulders, to be alive or dead—what is the difference?

Jack was certain she didn't know the answer, either, so she returned the shrug. The eleven others at the tables and the two at the bar gave him the most casual glance, even when the pistol had thudded on the wood, a large noise for so quiet a café, where the patrons spoke rarely and then mostly to their cuffs. The silence was her victory. By the second and most dreamy glass, Jack took a purple book from her jacket pocket and read with the calm of a person enjoying a triumph.

But when she was most calm, reading happily of the mother superior forced to chastise the beautiful young novice by flogging her bare shoulders as Christ watched on sorrowfully from his cross, André came to the table and, without a word, swiped up the pistol and sunk it in a pail of beer.

"Now, young man, or whatever is the thing you propose to be, please leave. Your friend Mademoiselle Ursula is always welcome, but you, with or without your weapons, are not."

Ignominious, that retreat, that little teary-eyed walk home. And, just as shameful, was to learn later that Vincent had been given the soggy pistol for safekeeping, ostensibly, but with the fillip that he should watch out for "boys" with big pistols lest she shoot a mouse. The pistol went under Vincent's thin mattress, where he could feel the iron lump in his dreams.

Not to the Bad Café, then. She would go directly to the train station and wait there for him at the platform, should he decide to run to meet her before the train took her away to Paris, for however long she did not know.

And run Vincent did, to find nothing but the station empty, the platform emptier. The posted schedule indicated that there was no train to Paris that morning, or to anywhere that day, until almost evening, hours away. He trudged back to the cottage, thinking she had returned, but when he called her name at the window, he received a quiet stillness for his answer. A neighbor's red cat, Nicolino, stretched along the doorsill, raising his head at Vincent's voice. He was the cat Ursula loved, feeding him at all hours a stew of fish heads and chicken hearts and leaving for him bowls of water on windowsills and along the garden path. A gutted field mouse dropped on her chest while she slept was Nicolino's occasional rewarding gift. Nicolino purring by her head until she woke and took the mouse from her chest and buried it in the garden beside the others. Nicolino attending the ceremony, his whiskers bristling and proud. Her man, who hunted to show her his love.

Vincent caressed the cat, but he was not encouraged to further caresses; Nicolino slipped his paw into the door's open crack, widening the space until he slipped his body through it. Vincent hesitantly followed him in.

Chapter 8

A s she had said she would in her letter, Ursula had gone to the station, only to find the waiting room closed and the platform and the scene empty, except for little puffs of red wildflowers edging along the train tracks, fragile and spiritual in the early light, a landscape made for Vincent. The gray rails in a gray dawn made her already miss home and the strange man who was expecting to find her there, asleep, as when he had left, and as if he had never left.

When she returned and found the cottage empty, she sank, worried suddenly that Vincent might be ill again, that he had left her that night rather than be ill in her presence, an animal whirling in foamy pain. Would he nick his other ear this time?

What she needed, and quickly, was to calm herself against the disaster. To calm herself, the better to care for him should he have hurt himself again. She went directly to her cache and found some empty vials and a syringe. She had not bought any morphine since she had last promised Vincent she would not, and now when she most needed it, she was left with nothing. She would go, she decided, despite the humiliation, to the Bad Café and find Louis and buy all the morphine in his stock.

The café was neither closed nor open, but in transition between the two. She entered, turned to the bar, and curtsied, ladylike, as if to the country curate. André took in the irony and appreciated it, reciprocating with a slight bow.

"He has left, Mademoiselle Ursula, not so long ago, but he has distinctly left."

"Which one of them remains, then, Monsieur André?" she asked politely, still savoring the qualification, *distinctly,* proving that André was always in charge, even with his diction.

Monsieur Louis was still about somewhere, if not at one of the tables in the back room, perhaps in the most rear location of all, in the little brick-walled garden behind the last door.

Mademoiselle was familiar with that garden, no? Having sometimes visited it and having sat some quiet time under the arms of the mulberry tree, white berries dropping sometimes on her while she slept in the shade, a book open on her lap, her mouth sometimes parted, sometimes to admit a vagrant butterfly or a bee diving for soft harbor. That same garden where she had often relaxed, Louis might be there himself reposing or counting his money or doing things men do when they see walls and wish to water them.

She turned quickly, saying nothing, walking briskly to the back room—vacancy itself—and, opening the narrow orange door, entered the garden. It was empty; the tree, table, and chair beneath it uninhabited, but she sensed a living presence, if only that of a cat behind the bush covering the wall. Maybe even Nicolino, who roamed the village freely, sometimes hunting for her at the café. Perhaps this time, instead of a mouse, he had Vincent between his teeth.

She peered behind the bush, seeing for the first time—though she could not imagine how she had never seen it before in all the time she had spent in the garden—a cleft in the wall cut to her size, a secret exit perhaps for those patrons wishing suddenly to quit the scene. As might have Vincent this very moment, too ashamed to face her anger before all the others, or perhaps, for reasons of his own, even Louis, whom she now wished urgently to see, her nerves twitching in their sheaths. Gathering up her dress, Ursula stepped through the opening, ready to surprise one or the other of the men, or at least to track the path of their escape.

Chapter 9

She stepped through the wall and came to me, and now she sleeps, my sleepyhead. I cannot count the hours by the days. (I feed her coffee and slices of bread toasted over the burner whenever she wakes.) All that sleeping was just sleeping away her past, and the Old World along with it, she said, when she finally woke to her new life. She always had told Vincent she needed a change, but how strange that change had come to her in this fanciful way.

And for me, too. My life became less lonely each hour with her. Seldom lonely, actually, because besides her company, I had my century to show her, starting with the radio in my kitchen. The radio, her first marvel—to listen to music at will, Beethoven's late string quartets and even all of Wagner's thunderstorms—and for free!—and the even more wonderful TV.

I had never owned one, but for her I bought a little set and a VCR on installment and planted it on a crooked table at bed's foot. Even with the one at home, I could not pry her away whenever we passed a shop with TVs flickering in the window. Eventually, she turned the color off, it was too vulgar, all that false, excited color. She concentrated herself on the black-and-white screen, fiddling with the contrasts and the shading, and, finally, finding that not compelling enough, she tried to freeze the moving images altogether and study the frames as if they were photos.

She could do that with videos of old black-and-white movies—there were so many of them for her to know, each, for a while, a little revelation. *Last Year at Marienbad* she viewed fourteen times, like shuffling photographs in hidden pattern, she said; Cocteau's *La Belle et la Bête* moved her, brought large tears to her eyes, especially when the Beast, returned from hunting in his gloomy park, his furry beast chest smoking, literally, with passion, whispers the word *Belle* in his swooning and unrequited love for the beautiful virgin imprisoned in his château. Ursula later regretted those tears, calling them shameful and absurd, and the sentiments that had engendered them criminal, born of a sickly and anachronistic conception of love—one of which she would eventually purge herself.

After a while, it was the static image she wanted, and the less movement within the picture, the better. "The story I'm seeking, Louis, is told in the space and light, and in the dialogue between them. This television is nothing but Eugène Sue and Victor Hugo," she said. "Just stories and stories—for children and invalids who must stay at home, for weepy people always waiting to begin their lives. I see that little has changed. This television is just like Vincent with his wholesome novels of the goodness displacing the bad."

What had she been watching? I wondered. Finally, she gave up the TV, and the videos, too—they were just talking photographs, illustrating simple stories.

Books. No end of them. Everything I had owned of fiction and poetry and art, though she left a book about Vincent in its place on the shelf, and, later, history from the end of her time to the moment of mine. She had no words for it, the twentieth century; it was beyond horror and beyond comprehension. Was she dreaming this, these books, those photographs? The slaughter of the Paris Commune in 1871 was a mere scratch on the shin of human history, nothing could be compared to what came after it. The wars, the Nazi camps, the Communist gulag. She looked at me one day very long and seriously, as she would at an intelligent ape on a park bench. Regarded me as if to ask, what was I made of, having been made from the stuff of this century? I was, we of this time were, so close to human—her simian cousin—but how had we come so far just to be so savage? So cruel?

Our art counted for something on the historical scale, I said, giving some weight to the better side of our humanity, bringing us to closer balance with the bad. She laughed. "Tell Vincent that," she said. "He would have loved to think of his paintings crossing the border into this murderous time, to help sweeten up its stink. He wouldn't have picked up a brush if he had thought it would have come to this."

And of twentieth-century fiction and poetry? She had gobbled up all the paperbacks I owned, and from there she went to the old library on Tompkins Square Park, sitting away the afternoons and staying fixed there, turning pages at the oak reading desk until I picked her up at seven to go for a coffee at De Robertis pastry shop on First and Tenth.

She knocked down espressos like shots of whiskey. To keep awake after all the reading, most of it fairly stupefying, the lazy reworkings of the literature of her time. It was Harriet Beecher Stowe—*Uncle Tom's Cabin,* Vincent's favorite—or Zola all over again, but not even as wonderfully sentimental as Stowe or as relentless as Zola. She was mad for Gertrude Stein and Wallace Stevens and Samuel Beckett, but she did not understand them very well, her English not adequate for their complications. Yet she did sense their spirit, she added, and knew she was cut from the same irregular cloth.

Yes, of course, there were others she appreciated, even admired—so what? She was shaking now. From all the coffee, I suggested, little cups and saucers lining the Formica-topped table. Nonsense!—it was from the emotions of her readings, from the strain of her concentration, and from the disappointment.

I tossed out some other names, hoping to quell her disappointment. She shrugged her shoulders. "Better not to read than to eat all that sugar, Louis."

Everything she liked was written mostly by men, I said. "And European types," I noticed.

"Who cares, Louis?" she said. "At the end of the end there are only books on the shelves, their titles and authors just ornaments on the spines. Books belonging to the common and anonymous store of the world's treasures, like communal grain and reservoirs of water."

She was reading and waking quickly to our time, without too much surprise at all the things I had thought she would marvel at: the light switch, skyscrapers, cars and buses and even airplanes overhead were of moderate interest; the telephone, just a toy. "If I do not go away, I will not need that instrument to call you," she said once, answering my defense of the electronic wonders of the day. "And when I'm away, what is more mysterious for you than to wonder where I am? More mystery and less talk, *n'est-ce pas?*" For all that, she did ask one day whether there was a machine to speak across time, because, you see, she might want to speak to him—you know—to relieve him of some worry.

The century brought her few excitements, but several regrets. She was disappointed that the West was won (a phrase she learned from a TV

Western); that the buffalo and Indians had all but vanished from their land, though once in a while she would suspect I had lied to her, imagining that the Westerns she devoured on the screen at Mousey's bar were in fact events of the day.

She pestered me about making a trip out there to Big Sky country, to the Badlands and the prairie and the Red River, where she could see for herself what had or had not happened to the West. Whatever was going on, the light there would be the best for her, she knew, because the wide space could hold more of it, all the fresh New World light still unsmeared with cliché.

I lent her the use of two cameras: the little Minolta and the old Leica that had cost me half my life. What things she could do with these extraordinary feathery machines, she said; with such shutter speeds and such film, she'd once and for all be able to squeeze time into light, to do, finally, all the work she had once dreamed of back there, in that sleepy century.

Now that she had her own cameras (three, including the ones I had lent her), nothing would stop her from her westward trek—certainly not me, though she had come to like me a lot, had even come to feel an ever-growing affection, but not love, of course, which she reserved for Vincent, who surely was back there waiting for her. Let him wait a while longer, I proposed. All the more to make him miss her and to treat her more respectfully when she one day returned. She gave me a look for the fool that I was.

A Diana she had bought. A plastic pinhole camera from a guy in the street. No meter, but she needed none, having, she said, an inborn feeling for the moods and temperament of light, its temperature, as well. She spent some morning and evening hours at the apartment window shooting into the East River and the vagueness beyond, shooting dawn and dusk lights and avoiding the full scope of the day. Her concentration was total, no hawk whirling over her head (mistaking her red thatch for its nest), no fire-engine siren breaking the air below could shake her concentration, leaving me to feel the nomad, pulled away from myself by the slightest breeze on the dune.

Half out the window, elbows on the ledge, camera out in space, she remained for whole long minutes, like some magnet gathering a dawn light only she and the Diana could fathom. But no sooner did day fully break, she retreated from the window to have her coffee and a little dry roll, and, with a little sigh of *ça suffit,* she returned to bed and to sleep, the sheet over her face—gone until the evening, when she woke without clock and rushed to wash and rush back to her station at window's ledge. Not too many days passed before she got tired of her labors, having used up their meaning, for it was the principle of the thing and not some relentless application she was after. Let someone else, after her, sit photographing dawn and dusk for every day of the year, let someone else with no ideas exhaust her ideas.

Now that she had given up her post by the window, she craved to be out there, below, free of all inhibitions, in the very streets where I saw mostly danger. ("Fearful of life, you are," she said. "So there is no life. Go die, fast, Louis.") I volunteered to join her in the city's wilds. But she needed to know the city by herself and I was not to come along, my being too much of a wall between her and the experience of the place, of experience itself, since I dreaded it so much, it seemed.

She soon went to all places in the city that gave on to rivers and great stretches of water leading to the ocean. She plied the Staten Island ferry, with its vista of the Narrows and the great Atlantic beyond. Later, she made friends with tug captains and crew, who, for the pleasure of her company, sometimes tugged her about on their watery errands up the East River across the Spuyten Duyvel and down the giant lumbering Hudson, her Diana trained on the edges of light sheeting the river.

Before long, she had exhausted the rivers, their bracing winds and dying lights, and had exhausted for the while her Diana. She had exhausted something in herself, too, though she was shy talking about it.

"Not ready, not ready," she would say when I asked why she had given up taking pictures.

"Not ready to speak about it?" I persisted.

"Nothing is ready, Louis," she said, finally, one evening as the sun was drowning in the Hudson and night was falling fast on us in the East.

We sat in the kitchen and pored over her photographs. There were some beautiful streaks of light, I thought, framed low on the print. Of course, she had sent them out for processing and so the results were far from what she would have done in her laboratory, where she would have carved the light right out of the darkness. But even with the prints that were before her she could tell the results would not have been what she had envisioned. And now the fear was that nothing in her equipment back there was the fault, blaming, as she had, the inferior technology of her time for her failures, blaming even the backward light of her century, reactionary as it was in almost everything, even in its collaboration with a modern and new idea of beauty.

Light not matching itself to the conception of the lens, light still thinking of itself living before the birth of the camera, still thinking of itself a painter's métier, belonging to artists straining to mix light's presence on a palette. What a tired collaboration, effete, a lie beyond its usefulness. Look at that charlatan Monet—what pretense!— as if the haystacks he painted at all hours of the day and evening had to do with anything but his own chromatic conventions. He need not have gone out to the fields to notice this or that effect in the changes of light; he might just as well have stayed home cozy in his slippers and calvados.

Look at Vincent! At least there was no pretense there—whatever the merit of his pictures. He went outside to paint because he could not stand to be indoors during the day, it made him shaky, and it weirded him—to use an expression she had just learned—all those four walls and roof and planked floor while the sky was out there. He should have been an Indian on the plains, with grass for his bed and the stars for his blanket. Vincent did not paint light, he painted his hysteria, which just happened to be interesting as painting.

She spoke a lot, sometimes. And when she did, I felt you could fall into her and take a long, long time before ever reaching her source.

She put her photographs away. That was that. *Ça suffit,* for the time, along with a lot of old things from the past she'd give a toss, like medicine bottles turned pale in the cabinet. Now it was the smoky nightlife she craved. Not just nighttime at Mousey's, which had soon become her family bar, everyone adoring her and her accent and her drinking. Mousey stood her more drinks that he ever had me. She liked the bar, so much like the one she habituated in Auvers-sur-Oise, the one Vincent called the Bad Café because every one in it looked so spiritually derelict and you always felt bad after you left it, your head aching from the raw drinks and the grainy smoke and the regulars' slack and miserable expressions. Vincent did not know how sweet they all were, that was all.

It was like him to exaggerate the Bad Café, as he did everything, his moods, his painting, his poverty, all in excess, his life an excess without stop. He had cut off a piece of his ear, imagine. He was nothing if he did not make an impression, his whole life in the service of making an impression. Who was there to impress? Not her! She exceeded him when it came to that. Do not let her renew that theme!

Mousey's was her familiar base and, therefore, it soon had become flat beer. To go there and do what? Sit at the bar and drink and watch TV and listen to the small talk—*toutes ces parlottes*? Ruby, the hairdresser of a small shop on Avenue C, who herself wore a dusty orange wig and who was always giving tips to Ursula on how to do tints and highlights on her red thicket; Lucco, who had been in prisons since he was seventeen, and who now, at seventy-three, was afraid to leave the bar stool to cross the street (the kids being so wild out there, "without the respect for nobody") unless Ursula accompanied him on his arm; and Mousey himself, a razor with pink ears, who knew where to buy brand-new tires and in-the-box TVs and anything else at huge discounts you casually might have mentioned you once had dreamed of buying or actually were in the market for, better than wholesale, if you were willing to go to Asbury Park, New Jersey, and see a cousin or two of his to get it. They and the others who formed the ancient nucleus of the bar loved her.

"They are the boring family I never had," she said one night on our way there after a kung fu movie in Chinatown. "They are assassinating me with their love. Is it that I have come all this way to be bored and assassinated?"

(No, I thought you had come just for me—to love me—I wanted to say, wishing she would answer: "Of course, Louis, mainly for that.")

She wasn't into the boredom business for very long, making new friends wherever she stopped, coming home one night with a bundle of teen-agers she'd met in Roosevelt Park edging the East River, my park. They called her Mama and Fren-chie and Pussy Pie. She laughed at everything they said and she roared at their jibes at me, the old dude, Father Time. "Ain't you too old for that Pussy Pie, man?" One of them sauntered about the kitchen poking into cups and jars. "Fuck, ain't you got any money, man?" That was Johnny Goat, a tall sixteen-year-old with a gold front tooth. She hung her arm about his skinny neck and looked at me with a grin, as if to say, "Is he not very great?"

She was very reserved back home, yes, you would not believe it, she was—ask Vincent—but here, somehow, that all had changed, the air of the times, perhaps. She was one of the roughs, she said, and like Whitman, she floated the streets, embracing equally the common blab of the pave, as the poet had called it, and the great silent voice of the Brooklyn Bridge. After all, art was life and life art. Only old Europe thought there was a dif-ference, and what was Europe now but a museum of its old bones?

The teenagers brought her to all the places where persons their age hung out at night, even though at nineteen she was the older woman, ancient to them, and being French helped to make her seem very old, like a lady. She went with them to places where I was forbidden, to clubs where only women went, and she soon reigned there, too; at home, the phone—the first one I had ever owned—ringing in the late afternoons for her, messages by the score on the answering machine, some supplicating, some tender and intimate, one or two bossy invitations.

"Ursula, did you get home OK last night, sugar? It's Jan, call me."

She never stayed out the whole night, wherever it was she went, but always returned to her Louis, a little drunk sometimes, and a little stoned sometimes, because now she was, anthropologically speaking, testing the drugs of our time.

"Ah! you should have known me at home, Louis. So serious, I was always so weighty, just perfect for that serious man I always talk about. I had no childhood back there, Louis," she lamented, but now she was really having her first wonderful youth. She had come to jump rope and play hopscotch in the far yard of the twentieth century, the streets her playground, and me, her sometime chaperon. *Amuse-toi,* I thought, but stay with me, where I'll watch over you for two hundred years, until the grave spits out my bones.

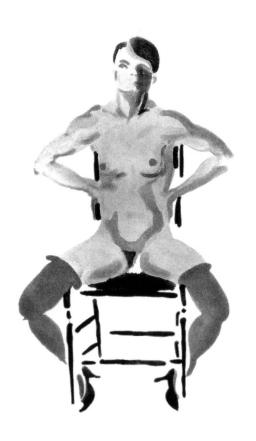

Chapter 10

One afternoon, she knocked at the door instead of just entering silently by key, unannounced, as she had always done, her presence a form of wonderful materialization.

"I have revised myself," she said, as I opened the door. Herself as a work of art, she explained— the final democratic ideal, everyone his/her own work of art, the body as canvas, the body as sculpture, the body as an arena in process, a show, a spectacle, one among the millions of spectacles. The New World had finally proved itself new.

At last, all gender differences and the discriminations attending them, all issues of talent—an idea so nebulous to begin with—all favoritism shown the young for merely being young (and thus no more than fodder for the sale and the creation of commodities, art being just one), all racial prejudices leading to suppositions of what race better created what art, all elitist and hierarchical categories had now and finally and forever vanished.

The flaming tangle bush gone, her head was now shaved to a red nub—like Vincent's in his self-portrait after he had razored his ear. Little lightning bolts cut down to the scalp above her ears. Four iron rivets climbed up each ear and a gold ring pierced her left nostril. Wait, that was not all.

A thin, blue-link chain circled her right arm. A starter, for soon she would get other tattoos, one inside her thigh, just for me; we'd design the image together. Then I would get one, too, the same image on the same spot on my person—for memory's sake. A souvenir of our friendship, also, because, as she explained, although we were lovers on occasion, we were at the heart, at the honest bottom of everything, friends—true comrades. My comrade, whom I loved and whom I missed at all counts of the minute, pretending not to notice when she was gone for very long into the night, doing her life, as she would say, while I waited for her to return, to return to do mine.

"What would Vincent think about these tattoos?" I asked. "Wouldn't he be jealous of the intimacy you and I have shared?" (As I, of course was of theirs.)

That was no problem. When, one day, she'd return home, and to Vincent, she'd show him these tattoos. She did not even have to make the demonstration herself, as he would undress her right off anyway, hardly she even got through the door, so feverish he would have become, having waited so passionately for her—and all of that.

And before he said a word, she'd ask him to get a tattoo inside his thigh, like hers, like mine, a symbol of the wonders of friendship extending beyond time.

No, he would not be jealous, not in the ordinary sense, not Vincent, once he understood that she was no different from the woman shipwrecked on an icy arctic floe far away and whose only companion was another shipwreck—and somewhat of an artist himself—and that the two had become comrades and sometimes lovers—as proximity and shared need not infrequently urges—but that at no time did she desert Vincent in her soul, where resides the sole source of all love such as theirs.

Fine words. She reserved their breed for me. Because with each day, and with her new friends, she had taken on her generation's lingo as spoken below Fourteenth Street.

"Where's my fuckin' boots?" she asked one morning, before she had even opened her eyes.

"How the fuck should I know!" I answered without thinking.

She enjoyed that. "Ah! Louis, you know how to play."

Along with her diction, she had changed her costume, too. The long white dress gone to the back-most reach of the closet, the pointy black lace-up shoes stowed in the darkness under the bed. Tight jeans and a gray tank top now covered most of her. Thick-soled, lace-up black boots took her everywhere.

I thought them ugly, cumbersome. She considered them the emblem of her—and her modern generation's—liberation from the fetish of the dainty shoe, designed by men to keep its pretty wearer enslaved to the drawing room, the salon, and places of fashion where men ruled. The Chinese bind women's feet, the Europeans encase them in paper-thin shoes—each culture insuring that women do not stray too far from the prison of home.

With her new clothes there was no longer any need for Jack. She could dress like Jack and still be Ursula, two in one, and vice versa. In fact, every woman in jeans and T-shirt was Jack, her brothersister, sisterbrother. She could saunter down the street in her boots, arm in arm with another Jack, and still be Ursula, whatever. (She took to the language so quickly.)

Gone, too, the quaint green overnight case and the fluffy stuff of her time that came crammed in it—lilac-scented handkerchiefs, bloomers embroidered with roses. Now she lugged a green shoulder pack, fed with maps, mace, Kotex, books of poems, her Whitman and her recent discovery, Sylvia Plath. She thought her poems weepy and stuffed with cotton, but she quoted them loudly, defiantly on occasion—mostly during TV commercials for perfumed soaps, youth-restoring skin creams, depilatories, menstrual-cramp reliefs, vaginal sprays, strawberry douches, and other products tailored for women, for their enhancement and their general well-being—to whoever was still awake in Mousey's bar.

Plath was good for the sentiments but not much for poetry. It wasn't at all better in her time, either.

Except for Whitman, the published poetry of her age sucked. That went for silly Baudelaire and his American uncle, E. A. Poe, and ditto the nerdy Rimbaud and the whole droopy British stuff.

"Did Vincent share your ideas?" I asked.

Vincent's taste generally could not be trusted. He had kept thrusting *Uncle Tom's Cabin* on her for its moral vigor, Tom, the greatest Christian since Christ. She preferred the coarsest pornography over it. Though Vincent may have been right when he said that they did not abolish slavery, they just perfected it. And just consider the painters Vincent had admired: Millet along with Gauguin; Monticello along with Pissarro; Vincent mixed it all up, the ordinary with the exceptional, but his judgment was correct about Baudelaire—for the wrong reasons though. That rebel poet with his bouquet of evil flowers was merely a poseur, a mama's boy playing the wicked man, and his verse just sugar with a black coat, expressing the tritest sentiments of the age— woman as whore-angel, and all that stuff that kept everyone confused and enslaved.

"You know, Louis, the whole of the late nineteenth century was a mistake. A *flop*." (She liked that word, pronouncing it to rhyme with *slope.*) Not that he mattered to anyone in his time, since no one but a few knew him or his work, but Vincent was a mistake and a flop, too. A misdirection leading to the false and dangerous roads of the twentieth century, that Vincent.

"What was it he had done," I asked, "to deserve this distinction?"

"He flaunted goodness as a principle in art," she answered without hesitation. "He gave your century another guise to elevate sentiment and to equate good intentions with quality. And look," she added, her mind following some tangent of thought, "at the murder you men have done in the name of noble intentions, more destruction in the first fifty years of your century than in the whole of the human world before. I'm so glad to be here, asshole."

We were sitting on a mountain-high pyramid of the century's murdered corpses, we were striding the pyramid's tip, looking out over the age of murder, when men had ruled and were still thinking of ways to cart the blood-stained pyramid over the frontier of the next millennium.

"You see, Louis, finally, Baudelaire's rotten bouquet and Vincent's wholesome sunflowers spring from the same male soil. A tired earth, Louis, fertilized by the boring shit of men's fantasy."

She was astride her vision, her head in her hands, her nose ring fluttering. She was one of the Indians exterminated by white men, and she was a Jew, too, murdered by white men. To be sure, all women were Indians and Jews murdered by white men, murdered by men of all color and manner of men, cocked and cockless.

She had shouted that one morning at Mousey's, when the sun was inflaming the windows. "That's all right, honey," Mousey answered, "take it easy. It sure beats working for a living."

"What am I doing here, Louis, with all these fools?"

"We can always find another bar," I said, apologetically, "maybe one a little more toward the West Village."

"Here! In your fuckin' century, I mean."

My century. The one I had invented all by myself, the fecal sunsets over the crematoriums, the mustard gas billowing like cotton candy over the body-jammed trenches, the pistol shots in the ear for those who proclaimed that poems were flowers and not engines of revolution. I was sick from my invention and wanted a drink. A thousand and one drinks and a quick bullet in the head for a nightcap.

"Was Vincent mediocre?" I asked, trying to bring the conversation to its earlier point.

"He was better than what I had told him. He was the best, but he thrived on rejections. Forever was he finding them, from both men and women. Even dogs did not come to him when he called, and cats looked away from him to search for their ghosts."

"And you, did you look away?" I asked, sad for Vincent and for myself.

"Only so that he would see me doing it and feel hungry, but never to look away in my heart," she said, as if explaining the obvious.

What did it say that she always looked at me directly? That unlike Vincent, I was not worthy of her feigned indifference, that her heart had space for only one concealed love and contained no room for me?

Her concealments, who knew what else they were, especially now that she was gone much of the day and night? My cameras and hers in the closet, up there on the shelf beside a box of her photos and a pair of my winter boots. What was she doing all day with all that open time?

"What do you do all day?" I asked, feeling low because I had to ask.

"Well, Bub," she said, winding up, "after I make breakfast for the menfolks, I clear and wash the dishes and get down to milking the cows, and when that's done, I just have enough time to get some of the house chores done, and, well, what with the mending and darning and sewing up quilts for the winter, there's hardly time to start getting supper ready for the hands, who come home mighty hungry after a day's work on the spread. Course, on Sundays, there's all those free hours after singing in the choir, but I reckon free time is just the devil's temptation."

"Well, better yourself keep busy then," I suggested, trying not to laugh.

She laughed—enjoying her own run—took her hands off her hips and threw her arm over my shoulder in a comradely way.

"Don't you see, Louis, there is so little space

left for you and me. You're a sweet man, like Vincent, but things have gone so far for so long that there is no way back for us—for women, I mean."

"All wars end, Ursula."

"But we are still in this one, Louis, even with sometimes peaceful men like you in the field."

That night, she came home very late. The sun was almost up and I was pretending to sleep, my unworried self buried deep in dreams purged of sadness. She came into the bed with a strange metallic smell on her breath and flesh, an old aluminum saucepan burned too many times and left forgotten on the stove. She sighed as if returned from a long journey, home at last and safe, and she dove into sleep. The morning passed and the afternoon, too. At about seven in the hot evening, I was about to leave and buy milk for coffee. An excuse to go out and not look at her breathing faintly and smiling to a cloud.

But she was waking before I reached the door, calling me very softly. She had been, she explained, for some while now, should I want to know, loving a wonderful drug. It kept her sleeping the deepest most warming sleep, warmer than anything, even me, who was her little stove, even Vincent, her furnace. It was those children who gave it to her, Johnny Goat, especially, he being the one who had shown how to prepare it in a spoon and how to do wonderful handiwork with a needle so that no traces of needlework were easily seen. Because here, you see, unlike in her time, this sort of pleasure is not allowed, and is punished, and so must remain hidden.

"Even from me?" I asked. Of course, because I was no different from Vincent, who allowed himself to drink but could not permit her to treasure her own happiness in her own way, he always preaching to her about holiness of the healthy body—made for activity and not for sleep, except when sleep was earned by the fruitful life of the day. What did he know, trembling, saving caterpillars from being crushed on the road, calling out to God from a ditch he had tumbled into after a night of drinking, painting all day, happy like a fox with a harem of voiceless hens.

I could not know that this wonderful drug was stronger and better than anything she had used before; perhaps it was the best invention this century had contrived—after all, even rocketing to the moon did not change the ugly feelings you took with you when you left the earth behind. She would have to find a way to take this wonderful stuff back with her when she returned home, crateloads of it, if she could haul such huge freight back through that strange wall. What changes that drug would bring to her time—quieting all that nervous male energy spent making wars and doing the rapine and bothering women with their aggressive masculine vanities.

Vincent would thrive, paint better, too, with the calm the drug would bring him. All that alcohol in his blood was just turning him into a pickled carrot. That wonderful drug of hers could change the course of the late nineteenth century, and thus of the whole of the sorry future, including the one in which I now lived. The Indians of the West would still be on their ponies and riding the plains, and all those Jews burned to ashes and all the madness brought by ideology and its vain, personal distortions (she had just been reading *Hope Against Hope,* Natalia Mandelstram's account of cruel imprisonments and her husband's slow death in a gulag for the crime of writing incorrect poetry) would never have happened.

"Sorrow everywhere, Louis."

"And love, too," I said, citing Vincent's great art and his passion for her as instances. And my love for her, as well, I added, feeling her slipping from me.

We went to Chinatown, Ursula thinking it would cheer her not to be reminded of white Europeans for a while, and she did cheer up for a while, until she got drowsy halfway through the garlic broccoli and started drinking cup after cup of black tea to wake herself up.

Across the room, eels entwined in a cloudy tank, and in another, five torpid carps gobbled fluorescent water. She was silent, studying her cup with a dreamy stare. Mine was the same, blue, a bridge over a stream, mountains brushed by mist, the standard Chinatown cup with the same tired landscape.

"Let's go," she said, awake and hungry for life again.

We walked down to the Brooklyn Bridge, crossing over it slowly, our arms about each other, stopping to kiss from time to time, the dark river and the sparkling city, the ferries and the tugs floating up at us on a wonderful July breeze. We stepped into Brooklyn and turned about to Manhattan, her mood taking the turn with her. Ursula took her arm from me, walking beside me, her arms dangling, head down, and shoulders stooping. Her soufflé had collapsed and now there was no wonderful breeze. I tried to hold her but she shrugged me off.

"Hart Crane jumped off this bridge," she said, accusingly.

"He jumped off a ship," I said.

"Right here, probably where we are standing. Because the world hates homosexuals and hates poets even more."

"Perhaps he was an Indian, too," I volunteered. She had not thought of that and asked whether I had any evidence for such an idea. I had none, of course, except to complete the fullness of her theme and for the sake of a mean joke.

"I will not trust you for these informations, and perhaps I will not anyway more trust you."

I wanted to say, Darling, I needed to wound you a bit, to mock you a bit and feel a bit superior because I have no power to make you love me enough, because nothing I do fixes you to me and makes you want me. Not just pride kept me from saying that; I knew that to plead with someone who does not love you is to sink, and I was already plummeting down to China.

When we got halfway over the bridge, all the lights of the city went dead and the ferries and tugs sank slowly into the East River, their running lights blinking off under the wet sea. She was going to leave me for a while to see some friends and to meet Johnny Goat and refresh herself with some of the stuff he was holding for her. Stuff she wanted very much, as now she was uneasy with the night and the bridge and all its dispiriting associations, and that Chinese food, too, so filled with chemicals that make you perspire and feel faint.

No, I could not come with her. And no, there was nothing I could say or do to stop her; better than me had tried to persuade her away from her pursuits and they never had succeeded, they just wore down to a nub.

We continued walking, bike riders zipping by singly or in friendly pairs, cars rushing in metallic rumble, their heat and rubbery gasses stinking up the walkway and rising to stink up the clean moon. I was walking too slowly for Ursula, on purpose, she said, so that she would not get where she was going—dragging my feet, is that not what I was doing? she asked. What a silly trick! She laughed at the childishness of my imagined ploy and took my hand.

"Do not worry, Louis. I will come back—don't I always come back?"

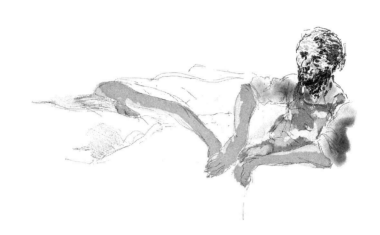

Chapter 11

I kissed her neck, holding her for some moments. It was better that she go ahead, I said, because now I was wanting to stay on the bridge and take it in a while more. She was pleased with me, giving me an extra hug, and then disappeared among bikes and lovers.

I wanted to stay, especially now that sunken ships and tugs were slowly resurfacing, swimming up from the bottom of the blackness, and the buildings again began blazing their lights, which were getting brighter all the time, so that the night began to look like a furious electric dawn rising. I began to shiver in the warm night, expecting my fit to come over me at any instant, me convulsing there on the bridge until the cables swayed and the roadways rattled down to the river below. Brooklyn Bridge is falling down. I hoped it would not fall until she reached the other side.

Vincent and I were drinking in the Bad Café. Two guys in love with the same woman. We decided to arm wrestle for her and clear things up once and for all. I told him how much I admired his art and that this contest had nothing to do with the esteem I held for him as an artist.

"Only *admire?*" he asked, ironically. "Why don't you just say you find it 'interesting' and deepen the insult."

"Well, it is interesting in a sentimental kind of way," I said. "Ursula had the right take on your stuff."

"Is that how you modern persons speak English?" Vincent asked. "So without dignity!—I can't imagine Ursula staying near you for an hour."

"Let's cut the crap and get on with the wrestling, Bro, so I can knock down your corny ass."

Arm against arm, elbows mashing into the table, we're at it. He's pretty strong for a thirty-seven-year-old geezer weakened by drink and eating shitty food, weakened by life's hurts, by the rejections of dog and cats, weakened by God's indifference, the whole of him weak except for his painting wrist.

"I'll twist your wrist off, fucker," I said.

Just then Ursula appeared and took us in with a glance. I could feel Vincent's arm relaxing a little, so I pressed harder. But he came back again as strong as ever. We were both looking at her and grinning a little boy's embarrassed, proud grin.

"This is for you, baby," I said.

"Tea at five, dearest, as usual," Vincent added.

She smiled and nodded to us politely. "Is it that Louis is here?" she asked, turning to André.

He jerked his thumb in the direction of the back room and continued scouring the zinc counter.

"I'm here," I said, "not back there."

"Yes, thank you, but it is the authentic Louis I'm searching for," she said, giving me and Vincent a friendly pat on the shoulder as she walked past us.

The light was really getting bright now, but just around me. I tried to rise from the floor and maybe grab a bridge cable so that I could swing home and land right in bed. What golden light— and right before my eyes.

"You OK, Bro?"

It was Johnny Goat and his gold tooth gleaming at me in the night. Ursula was there, too. She had returned with the Goat in tow because I had look so weird to her before she had taken off.

"Like an ost," she said.

Like a *host*?

"Like a fuckin' *ghost,* man," Johnny explained. "Don't you get the way she talks?"

They took me home in a cab and settled me under the covers. In the kitchen, the two giggled and whispered a lot and talked their drug mumbo-jumbo until I heard the door shut and felt Ursula in bed beside me. She had that burned-aluminum smell again. She let out a few sighs and nestled her head on my chest, her arm flung around me. I tried not to move so that she wouldn't wake, but no matter how much I tossed and turned, she didn't wake, her thin body seemingly filled with cold lead, her arm alone some two hundred pounds. I kissed her lips and tasted aluminum spittle.

I closed my eyes and tried to think of soothing things to help me to sleep. In the beginning, I could only see the Ursula I first met, her body golden and her hair a wildness of red tangle and thicket, Ursula in the kitchen tub and the soapy water trickling down her shoulders and breasts. Thinking of her made me happy, but I was not calmed.

The Ursula beside me was so far from the one I had met that hot afternoon, and she was going further. So was I, myself, so far from myself, back to my young days when I drank martinis at Madame Porte's café and Art Moderne pastry shop. The triangular glass chilled, the beads of chill sliding down the stem to the chilled base; serpentine lemon peel draped slumberingly along the iced rim, the gin and vermouth smoky and sluggish from the cold; a green olive napping on its side in the deep burrow of the glass—the perfect martini. Plato's martini. I dream of it still, along with triangles, justice, and beauty.

All the drinking, all the time, everywhere. For a while, when I was flush, I drank at the oak barroom of a fancy hotel, loving it most in winter when snow tipped the trees in the park across the street and I could stare at the whiteness and feel myself sinking into its warmth, sleeping 'til spring in an igloo nestled in the park. I drank in the bar's soft leather armchairs, the little polished black table holding up my drinks for me. Scotch it was then, for winter, single malt smelling of peat and smoke, a most hearty broth of the glen.

Francis, the barman imported from Paris, smiled at me from time to time. I tipped big for that smile, thinking it most elegant to be recognized by certain barmen. I drank until I was too tired to get up and go elsewhere for dinner, and stayed at my table with a cold club sandwich and a half bottle of red wine. A brandy or two following. Or three. The customers changing from afternoon to evening faces. Francis, my closest friend, looked at bit haggard and bored, myself ready to fold there on the spot, the table my bed, the tablecloth my sheet. But I managed a glorious exit, bigshot tips sprawled on table and bartop.

"*Bon soir*, Francis."

"*Bonne soirée, monsieur.*"

Clinging, clinging to the last moment before going to sleep, some brandies later in bed, to that "*Bonne soirée*" and the suggestions of warmth I had credited it.

Then the morning wonderment. How did I get home? Thinking, thinking, and retracing my steps from bar to street, and then, nothing. A miracle. Monsieur had alighted safely in bed as if descended from his cottony taxi cloud. Fancy stuff. Gentleman's stuff. Not like the souls on the Bowery shouldering the walls of greasy buildings.

Not, until later, like the ones drying out in the public wards, strapped to a cot, hands shaking, the lips blue, the eyes set on a snowball in Alaska or on a pinhole in the Milky Way. "God, if you are there, a drink please."

She wakes in the night, her face pressed up to mine. "Louis, let's do the thing," she whispers tenderly. She tongues my nipples, her stubble hair whisking my chest in a gentle slide.

I kiss her with all the history of my waiting for her to walk through that wall and into our life. She returns the kiss dreamily but then, as if recalling something, she stops abruptly and props herself up on an elbow.

"But no penetration, Louis."

No, there was nothing wrong; nothing at all wrong with her and nothing that I could do to change her feelings. Because now she had come to learn what she had only sensed by intuition back there in her half-awake time, that all male penetration was a form of invasion and that all such invasions carried with them the history of all male invasions—whether amatory or military—with their subsequent conquests, pacifications, subjugations, and colonizations. She could no longer bear such imperialism from a man—or from a woman who had internalized such male ways—now that she understood sex in its historical context.

"Oh," I said, dampened. "Will you also demonstrate this information to Vincent, should you return?"

This was a difficult question. Because, having only reached the fullness of her idea in the twentieth century, it might not be correct to impose its consequences on a man so completely bound to his backward time. But she would consider the issue before springing it on him, *fait accompli;* she owed him that.

We kiss again, and at first touch cautiously, with the little cloud of theory puffing over the bed to keep us on guard. But soon the steam and breezes from the bed send that cloud for a spin out the window and high and far from us, floating out there over the Brooklyn Bridge and sailing on its way to lofts in Brownsville.

"Let me love you, and let me be the wonderful drug you love," I whisper.

She smiles at me in a drowsy calm, the sweet after-love sleepiness.

"You are a sentimental old fucker, aren't you?" she says faintly, smiling, entering the gate to sleepland.

"*Au revoir,* Vincent, I kiss you," she says, shutting the gate behind her.

Chapter 12

I'm soon, too, in dreamland, where I live a good life, in that Bad Café where I could drink marc and calvados and suckle Ursula's lactating breasts, oozing creamy green Pernod, the poisoned milk, which now would never harm me. I woke, who knows what hour. The morning of the next day or the next month, the last black dawn of the century. Blackbirds fleeing from a pie, as Vincent cuts it into thirds with his painting knife. A stream of blackbirds flying to the sun.

"What was he like?" I had asked her one day, almost believing her Vincent story was true, that she was indeed a waif of time and had come to me through that brick wall from a summer day in 1890.

"For a man so lonely, he had a wonderful, reassuring self-sufficiency," she said, finding it odd that of all his qualities, it was that which first came to her mind.

"He wrote most of the evenings, even when we were together. Letters to his brother but to others as well, to friends—he has a beautiful, plain style," she added, if his letters to her were evidence—she always carried one or two of them with her wherever she went, she may have had a few in her green bag she'd read me one day. Even if he went drinking alone, without her in the Bad Café, he wrote and made little sketches, on the letters themselves sometimes.

No matter what he did or how much he drank at night or if he stayed up reading one of those enlightening novels he was always reading and even if they made love the whole of the night, he'd wake at the merest suggestion of morning's approach, waking just before dawn itself and he'd heat up whatever leftover there was from the night before, some weak tea or coffee, and he ate whatever was at hand, some roasted chickpeas in burned oil, a salted sardine, crusty bread, or sometimes nothing. Even when he stayed at her cottage he ate little, though there was plenty of food waiting—some cheese and fruit and eggs she had set out for him. He just wanted to leave and start painting.

For the whole day, raining or burning hot, he was out there on some terrain he had chosen on his strolls or on his way to a place he was painting; he always knew in advance the spot where he had intended to work, knew the angle of his easel on the site, the size of the canvas he required for the job. He had dreamed about that stuff all night; even while he was writing letters or drinking or making love to her he was dreaming about painting.

He left his inn or her cottage as the sun was starting its day, and then that was the end of him until nightfall and even beyond its fall, when he'd put candles on his hat and cheat the darkness.

Would you call that an interesting life? He had never traveled—yes, once to England to work in an art gallery and to learn to drink tea—in the sense of having taken a journey to some place unusual, interesting, or frightening. And he went to the Borinage coal mines where he suffered more than the miserable miners, probably the happiest time of his life, he could feel so saintly, and had lived in France, of course, where nothing French—because it was French—interested him. He had no visible friends, hence all the letters, and no society except for Dr. Gachet and herself. He liked Gachet but shied away from him. And her? To see him live was to think that he did not need her at all, except that he needed her above all.

He was impervious, that Vincent. One day, they were out in a field, the one near the Romanesque church. She had taken a blanket and a basket of delicious trifles to eat and drink the day long—a bubbly cider and truffle omelettes among some of the delicious items she had prepared that morning—and she had Zola's novel *Nana* to read—on Vincent's recommendation—to keep her engaged for the while, wanting to spend the day beside him, under a red umbrella, and watch him and fall asleep when she chose. In short, she had chosen to be the happy one for that day.

Well, to say that he never gave her one glance is to count one glance too many, his painting and painting all the time, just as if he were in the hospital courtyard with the crazy loons circling him—indifferent to them, impenetrable to her. That was the best time. He was so apart that she believed nothing she'd do would ever reach too deeply into him or ever hurt him beyond repair. It let her breathe, that; let her feel free, never to have to mind her manners, so to speak, and what is more inducing of love than the obdurate soul of the other who loves you but erases you and returns wholeheartedly to work the moment you leave to buy bread or to betray him—or her.

Late that afternoon, when a chill swept through the open field, he left the painting and went off to pee behind a tree. When he returned, he threw himself down beside her and held her very tightly, taking the wind from her.

"I've thought of you all day," he said. "Missing you, missing every instant away from you."

He kissed her eyes and face, his body actually trembling—though that was not so unusual—shuddering, you might say, for love. Yes, he had forgotten to button his trousers and his leaky thing was rubbing up against her in the growing dark. And all the while she knew he was thinking of returning to the painting, which was getting cold in the night.

I reviewed these stories until morning, when she woke, with her smile gone. She had a very sad dream and I was not there to catch her falling into it, having abandoned her for a drink, probably at Mousey's—so would I please now hold her until she was fully awake and had cohered herself into a person.

I kissed her and walked her to the bathroom and rinsed her face with a soft cloth and left her there on the pot while I made coffee and heated the milk and opened the window to let in the new day.

And the bad dream? I asked.

Well, she said, giving a little shudder, in this dream, she was flying above Auvers-sur-Oise, and she could see everything beneath her, but she herself was invisible. The town hall and the Bad Café, Vincent's inn and the Romanesque church were there solid as ever, and so, too, her little cottage, but ill-tended, her red path crawling with snails and lizards and overgrown with coarse grass and rusty weeds. When she came down to earth, she found her laboratory shed in ruins, chemicals spilled over, corroding the worktables and biting into the floor, photographic plates in splinters everywhere, her giant cameras fallen to the ground with their crowns broken.

The cottage windowpanes hung in knife-shards, and her front door strained on its hinges.

All the plates and silver, all the pitchers and vases had vanished from the kitchen; the table was turned over, sacks of turnips and potatoes sat between its spread-open legs. Two of Vincent's paintings—a field swaying in the chalky rain, her garden with red sleeping cat, Nicolino, at his siesta, done for her nineteenth birthday—were stuffed one atop the other against a broken window. Ghastly, all this vandalism. Who could have done such a thing?

She had seen enough, and she flew to the Bad Café, expecting to find Vincent, but the café was deserted; sheets draped the bar and tables, as the establishment was clearly in the process of being painted. Only one wall still kept the familiar smoky brown hue while the others shone bright orange.

How queer the place looked in daylight with all the windows open and all the light of the day reaching far in to the farthest corner of the room. A few hospital beds were all it needed to convert the café into a ward, a few pots of red roses scattered here and there for a touch of healing nature to complete the hospital aspect.

She and Vincent could go there for rests from life, when her cottage and his inn grew too oppressive, when waking and putting on shoes in the morning took too much effort and making the morning coffee took the entire day, the work in grinding the beans alone taking three hours, and add another three for the water to boil.

There'd be only the two of them in the ward,

just the two in the same giant bed sleeping and eating dates and having their pulses taken by nuns in strict nurses' habit, the same sweet sisters who tucked them in at night—no later than ten—and waked them at daybreak for tea and toast and prayers. "Praise life," Vincent would say, his only prayer, now that he had left Jesus to join with all the other gods who lived in trees and sifted through winds and seas.

Not in the cottage and not in the café, leaving only a field or a hill, some outdoor place where Vincent could be, painting away in the bright day. But he was in no field whatsoever, no open-air corner of the town, no garden filled with weeds and wild red flowers. As long as the sun was still up, Vincent hated being indoors in whatever weather, even in the rain, but it was her last hope, so directly to the inn she went, flying there in no time, even with a little stop back at the Bad Café just to be sure she had seen what she had seen—the orange walls and the empty rooms—and flew up to Vincent's attic window, standing outside it as if on a ledge in space.

There he was, or some version of him, a huge reddish cat in trousers and open white shirt, his face bewiskered and red-furred up to his round blue eyes, seated (where was his tail?) in the room's only chair, by the window, his cat's head and one pointy ear tilted toward the light—toward her. Broken paintbrushes and twisted tubes of oil paint lay writhing about him on the floor; easel legs jutted out from the iron stove's open door, and a painting knife, handle missing, stood on its tip, trapped in an open jar of honey drying on the windowsill.

Wisps of bluish smoke curled up from his chest, his body burning slowly from the inside, his heart and lungs exhaling the aroma—received even through the shut window—of chestnuts roasting in a wintery park. His eyes were fringed with a soft animal gum where old tears had collected in the fur, though for the moment there were no tears flowing, his eyes dry and reflecting the clouds behind her.

"Beauty," he sighed. "Beauty."

"I'm here," she said, "come back for you." But he could not hear or see her, the breath leaving him, an old red cat dying in a wooden chair by the window.

Chapter 13

"Beauty," Ursula said, still hearing his voice through the window of her dream. She caressed my face, reassuring herself that indeed she was now here with me.

"It was so sad, Louis, his dying for want of me."

"Yes," I said. "He was the kind who would die from want of you."

"And I of him, too," she said defiantly. "I am made of that kind." She waited for me to agree.

"Of course," I said. "We are all three cloths cut of that kind."

She did not welcome my inclusion and she shrugged her shoulders to remove the weight I had just placed there.

"Peut-être," she answered, looking away perhaps back into her time and home or thinking about that wonderful drug she would shoot into her century to pacify it.

"What happened to Vincent?" she asked.

"He shot himself," I answered, with a certain meanness in my heart for her.

"Pas possible," she said, trying to hold back her surprise. "He would naturally miss."

"Well, his aim must have improved after you left him," I suggested.

Ursula went up to the window and spoke to the pane.

"Of course, that will not happen, Louis, because I will return to him and see to it."

"Perhaps you could also bring him over here for a visit and let him see what he would have missed."

"Into this filth?" She laughed. So did I.

I was mistaken, in any case; it would not be for Vincent alone that she would return. To abdicate herself for a man—that would be a capitulation of everything she believed in, and sentimental, too. No, she would return to set things straight, to correct her century at its pivotal moment, starting with her and Vincent, to let him see that there was no reason to kill himself, personal sadness being reactionary and self-indulgent, a luxury that the poor could ill afford, he least of all, with his one pair of broken boots. Let the unproductive rich kill themselves and one another; artists, especially, had no time for the suicide business.

She'd return to her time and then she and Vincent would go forward on the matter of life, she taking care of him until he woke from his melancholy; perhaps she'd build a little glassy cabin for him—so he'd always feel himself outdoors—on her property and a cozy studio in which to hang his easel and brushes.

That was a good plan, and she would get busy about it as soon as possible, tomorrow perhaps or the next day, she said, tapping the cleft between her left thumb and forefinger, her newly favorite pin cushion; but right now, she needed to see a certain goat about a horse, because she was worn out from dreaming and she needed a rest, needed to prepare herself to feel good again before making off to join Vincent, who would want to see her at her best and most calm—he deserved that, after all that missing and waiting for her.

"He may not want you back," I suggested.

She laughed. "Dream on, Louis."

"And you may not be able to get back," I added. "Time moves forward," I said with authority. She gave me all her sleepy attention.

"We know that time's atoms move in a progressive direction and, like rivers, flow only ahead and to the great ocean and central pool of time, where it collects itself to refurnish eternity."

"Really?"

"Yes, and in space, when time on occasion does reverse, its atoms disintegrate, causing huge explosions and fires the size of stars."

She gave me a quizzical look. "Well, Louis, I'll check all this out one day before I leave."

But for now, she was only taking a short trip, to meet the Goat and other kids, and she would return soon, don't worry, to her brilliant Louis.

Vincent would have to wait for her a little longer, but not much longer. A little smudge of a kiss on my lips, a little caress on my face, and she was gone to her private streets.

I left, too. For a consultation with Dr. Paul Gachet on Fifth Avenue at Eighty-second Street. I expected Vincent's portrait of him was still hanging there at the Metropolitian Museum where I had last seen him years earlier, his head pensively in his hand, looking directly at me, a branch of foxglove, the symbol of his homeo-pathic vocation, soaking beside him in a jar of water. Mine was a professional call, me needing advice from the doctor himself, the mender of the wayward and the distressed. Vincent once had sent Ursula to him, hoping the doctor would find ways other than morphine to calm her, invent some bracing and uplifting herbal tonic for her body and spirit.

She went to satisfy Vincent, to prove that she had tried, out of regard for him, to alter herself. Dr. Gachet, sweet to her as always, as when he had come to her as a child, she sitting—a red wool scarf wrapped about her neck—on a stool, reading silently by a window, or at age eleven, lying in bed burning with rheumatic fever, a book of Baudelaire's poems clutched in her hand.

Awkward, at first, shy, too, his eyes drooping as he asked her various intimate questions con-cerning her appetite and sleeping habits, the reg-ularity of her menstrual cycles. He had her extend her hand and spread out her fingers, which remained steady as he looked into her mouth and studied her tongue. He examined the moons of her fingernails and the irises of her eyes, and finally, he fingered her hair, sniping off a twig and burning it in a petri dish, where he studied the ashes.

And, as often when she was a child, he found nothing amiss. She was healthier than health, more vigorous than vigor, she was a sound young woman, except, of course, for some random and inexplicable bouts of nerves.

"Of course," she said. "So how did Dr. Gachet explain," she asked, feeling warmly to him now that the formal interview had ended and he was once again her old friend, why she, while reading a book she enjoyed, a simple book and in no way unnerving or while in her garden quietly photographing a veined leaf under the great calm of the sun-filled day, or why while doing anything not disturbing or disquieting or troubling, she would suddenly feel her heart pound and her breath go short, her breathing like the panting of a Labrador after a long run through a dark forest? Why did she feel her skin shrivel and, worse of all, experience a great weakening and a sinking into the earth, down into long earthy tunnels, the encrusted roots and tendrils of trees hanging damply above her head, the earth itself so dark and specked with glittering minerals and smelling of burned cork and chilly cellars and she falling into it forever?

"Coffee," he said. "Did she drink it?"

"Only with Vincent," she answered. So drinking coffee did not explain why fits had come over her before she had ever met the painter.

He turned to her slyly. "Did Jack have these fits, too?"

"He, too."

"Did Ursula have them more in the company of men than with women?"

"More in the company of fools," she replied tartly.

He took the insult, quickly loading his pipe until it was so packed he could not draw smoke. She apologized. He deeply apologized. There was friendly silence, in which she went to the open window: the hills, the streets, the rich dark trees, the footbridge across the drying stream, the Romanesque church, the town hall with its tricolor waving from a mast in its head, Raveoux's inn with a sprinkling of iron tables on the terrace, the Bad Café and its mulberry tree.

Calmness, the whole meaning of her century, of her Auvers-sur-Oise, and she, too, calm and thinking of Vincent and imagining the two of them in her thick garden lying side by side, reading, while Vincent turned and slowly stabbed the sleepy juice she loved into her inner thigh.

"It is not because it calms these fits that I love morphine," she said, turning to the doctor. "No, I love morphine, and we love each other."

"Can a substance love?" the doctor asked, his face inclined to hers, his voice soft, fearful.

"It loves me."

"More than Vincent?"

"Naturally."

"More than God?"

"Morpheus is a god," Ursula said, "and he will outlive you and me and Vincent."

I stared at the museum wall where Gachet's portrait had once hung, his expression, Vincent wrote, a model of nineteenth-century melancholy. The doctor had left the museum, a guard informed me, his portrait recently auctioned and transported to Japan, perhaps, whose art Vincent had so admired. I had come all that way uptown to miss the doctor by some months. It was not for Ursula that I had made this pilgrimage above Fourteenth Street, where the uptown winds lift your heels to the crowded sky, but to have the doctor verify the sad rumors of my heart.

Chapter 14

" If I stay here much longer, I'll be sucking cocks for dope," she said.

And worse. She pulls down her jeans. Look at her thigh! Black and blue and purple, a bruise the shape of Brooklyn. It happened while I was gone. She'd fallen with a needle in her arm and woke up three hours later, needle still stuck in her arm and a baby lagoon of drying blood on the bathroom tile. Shit! It was horrible, frightening, the fuckin' worst thing that had happened to her yet.

But she was never going to let it happen again, *jamais.* "Fuck, man, I don't want to die like that." She shudders—seeing herself dead stuns her imagination. How could she ever let things go that far?

She looks at me. "Louis, please, honey, go get my cameras back."

"Which ones?" She had sold them all one morning while I was out.

"All of them. So you go now and do that nice thing for me."

Leica, Minolta, Diana, a cardboard box with a pinhole for light, whatever it was she'd shoot with it. ("I shoot and I shoot and I shoot," she once said. She was a marksman and could shoot the buttons off your fly, could shoot any camera, and of course—the wide smile—she'd shoot you-know-what into herself.) I was ready to go off on my knightly mission, retrieve her gear to get her on track again—shoot film, darling, and keep your arms smooth and pure.

Pawnshop tickets. None, of course. She had unloaded her cameras in the street. The Nikon for a bag. The Leica for whatever. Where gone to, then? To a guy in the street near the boccie field on First and First or maybe B and Houston, to the Goat's skinny friend, Juanito Shoes or Juan-the-whatever.

I could have searched to the stretch of nine days and nights and never have found those cameras and it would never have mattered if I had.

"Well, they were really for you, anyway," she said. To get me to thinking about myself again, and what I would do with myself after she had gone, because she *was* going and had thought it simpler, more tender, *tu vois,* if I were not home when she left.

She had already packed while I had slept the innocent night away and had left me a large, flat, yellow box with all her photos—her errors—in it and a handwritten good-bye note, too. Already packed. I was spared the folding of the T-shirts and white panties and the laying out of the three flat white bras.

I'd leave with her, I said. If she was falling, I'd join her in the fall. Fuck the hope-filled dawn and the responsible day. I'd join her there at the edge and backward rim of childhood and death. I'd buy a syringe so big you could kill a whole zoo with it, larger than a veterinarian's giant needle, and shoot tequila. White in my left arm, gold in my right. Then we'd sit in my park on the East River and look at the tugs until our souls sailed off with one of them, leaving our bodies to rot on the slatted park bench, leaving those shells behind us once and forever.

Our spirits would hitch a ride on one of those passing tugs and we'd get off at the Narrows and sail away to all the territories between life and extinction. The map was large.

"I must go alone, now," she said.

"Go where?"

"To Vincent."

She puts in her case that Chinese cup we bought on Orchard Street the day we got the red-and-black linoleum carpeting for the kitchen. We made that kitchen shine for a week. She giving it the high-polish rubdown, her ass doing a little shimmy in her functional cotton panties from the Republic of China, her voice deep keyed, smiling at me, singing, "Honey, honey, honey, come bring me dat money." Where had she learned that song?

"Yes, I miss him. I went out on him and now I feel bad."

"And me?"

"I'll miss you, too, differently."

She went out on him. Where had she been with me? Neither with him nor with me, but as my visit to Dr. Gachet would have confirmed for me, always with the third and strongest rival, whom she dreamed about day and night, in every climate and latitude, in every zone of time.

"I must go back to him," she said. A wonderfully mean look came over her. "He's delicate, that Vincent. And he must miss me, too, the way I stride and swivel him, like no woman has, not even those brothel nags he sometimes mounts."

She understood my expression and came up close and put her arm about my neck. "Forgive me, dear Louis."

"Honey, don't go," I said.

What a thing to ask of one who has already left, gone down so far back in years, her green suitcase in hand, her slim body ready to slip over the border of the century. I sit awhile thinking of her, everything suddenly so calm, after the door had shut and the footfalls died in the stairs— the coffee, a pond in my cup, the sky, a blue cutout glued to my open window and reaching out as far as the Brooklyn Bridge. The whole of my world calmly winnowing down to a lost bear returning to her red pot of honey.

And now I'm also down the stairs and in the street, turning corners, looking for her. I wave to

Mousey as I pass his window and give a grudging salute as I pass Ursula's stable of dealers, who wonder, if, hey, man, she's moving to another town, doing a fuckin' geography on a Greyhound, 'cause that little bitch sure move her ass round the block, she move it, she shake it, she swivel it, she grind the basement of hearts all the way to the other side of China.

"Hey, man, where she go? I think she left you, Bro. She split on your straight ass."

In a flash, I'm at the old field of rubble where we had met. She's there, too, poised to enter the wall, one leg already disappearing through the opening slit. She turns to me with an affectionate smile, a smile of love and regret, and slides through the wall and steps into a garden. Now she's at the back door of the Bad Café, a bright mellow light flashing as the door opens, and then a matte darkness as the door closes and the wall seals and the century shuts down behind her and me forever.

I run to the wall, wanting to rush through and catch up and join her, but I find no opening and nothing at the wall's base but a pair of old jeans, a T-shirt, a needle.

Chapter 15

Following the red cat, Vincent stumbled through the unlocked door of Ursula's cottage. Empty the living room and empty the kitchen beyond and even more empty of her was the bedroom, where a bouquet of lilies of the valley burned whitely on the night table. He returned to the living room, where they first had met, his eyes blinded momentarily by the brilliant tondo of light on the floor's center. And there, in the inmost target of the light, lay a reddish pelt. A fox cub snatched from its lair, the animal fresh with life, still soft and smelling of pine needles and clouds drowned in streams.

A woman's pubic pelt it was, all the rest of the human animal blanched out in the blazing light of reversed time. Her body, her face erasing into the obliterating wash of light even as Vincent, kneeling to the floor, came to recognize that face as Ursula's.

Scattered in the pale shadow of her once-human form were Ursula's artifacts: a plastic wristwatch; a roll of 35-mm black-and-white film still in its plastic container; shards of a blue Chinese cup; a red buffalo nickel. Vincent pocketed the relics and souvenirs of Ursula's recent life.

She had been ahead of him, always. Now he was again in the rear. But he could not and would never catch up, now that he was emptied of himself and weightless, except for the ballast of her souvenirs. There was so little of him left, now that he had indeed become a shell of Frankenstein's creature, a sunken shape without life to give it stuffing.

She was always the fast one, the first one. Her art somewhere else, out of the moment, while his art troubled the moment, like a child chasing a frisky cat in a walled garden. He wanted to catch everything that sped—the chalky rain speeding down a yellow field, the sun fanned by the silvery breeze of olive trees—and to keep the living moment of it living, while she sought permanence and fixity everywhere—light and shadows, her imperishable pyramids.

He left the cottage and, crossing the tangled path, shutting her garden gate behind him, walked rapidly to his lodgings. Pure was the sky, an icy sheet caught in a sun of pale Dutch butter. Vincent thought of a painting he'd make of it, of the sky and the whirl twisting in it, a painting that would capture alive this day forever, taking in all its dispositions, taking in even the vanishing density of the morning.

But the sky and the day it covered, so vivid in

other particulars, had been misinformed of his feelings, or had not noticed them, reflecting none of his sorrow in the tiniest mote of light. It was an incomplete day, with blank passages in its portrait.

He was home now, under the wooden shroud of his wooden roof. The small square window letting out to the sky and the park, opened to the shouts of happy children in the schoolyard, crows screaming in a field of Sundays. The sky still had no news of his grief, waiting for him, unchanged, to paint it. He would make the completion, paint the bright day and imply its sorrows, a chill of shadows crossing a field of mown hay. He'd rob the day of itself, taking its fullness with him on a canvas to the bottom of his windowless grave.

He had never painted or sketched her. Not from lack of wanting, not from forgetfulness or neglect. He had thought, in some superstitious way alien to his usual thinking, that each day he forestalled painting her assured them another day of life together, postponing their illness, their fatigue, their aging, their death. She had never taken a photograph of him, nor had they ever had one taken of themselves together. But, then, she had never photographed any human thing, or any animal, and she always had said that she needed no visual remembrance of their friendship.

She would never forget him, and she judged there were not enough years left in his life to forget her in the distance of time. All the same, he was already obliterating her, her form was disappearing, as it had on the sunlit floor. Face and body going away from him, melting away into time. Of all of her, he did recall most strongly some strokes and arcs of light on obscure paper surfaces, her art. Why, now that she was gone from plates and paper, could he see her reigning through their difficult beauty?

See her reigning, and waiting for him with a little smile of triumph. For all his weightlessness, he might still catch up to her if he hurried; she, there, having scouted the territory and waiting for him, impatient for his long visit. For him, now, only his visit mattered, the rest of life just packings and preparations.

He reached under the mattress and drew out Ursula's heavy revolver, so absurdly cumbersome and ancient and beer smelling that Vincent laughed—and went out again into the road and walked past the town hall and many solid houses until he came to a quiet farmyard across from an open hayfield. There he nestled himself against a little hill of hay and dry manure, settling himself in as if about to take a refreshing siesta.

There, from his straw crib, he envisioned many things, even the slanting snow as it would fall over him in two hundred years, its water trickling down to the ash that once was him, the little powdery remains of him mixing with the snow that had changed into water fallen from the sky covering Auvers-sur-Oise, and this snowy water washing down through the pores of the rotting wooden box that held him in the earth, and taking himself—his very last pinch of human dust—to dissolve away into the grave's narrow patch, itself only a plot in the wider earthy world, a particle in God's room.

The day was finally completing its true likeness, filling in its blank passages with Vincent's black news. Now Vincent winnowed his gaze to the open field and sky, where squadrons of crows swooped along green alleys of mown hay. Above the yet uncut stalk tips, nineteen crows hovered, describing, in glistening black formation, the letter "V."

"V" for Vincent and the lonely vapor of his soul already sensing its journey to a yet lonelier room where souls wait their turn before vanishing forever into the great soul of the world.

The thud of Vincent's bullet was so soft that only those crows closest to him bolted skyward, their cries rising as the shot's echo started its redundant course.